THE AFFAIR BOX

THE AFFAIR BOX

PECO GASKOVSKI

Published by Walking Path Press

www.walkingpathpress.com

ISBN 978-0-9920527-4-4

Cover photograph of Michelangelo's Dying Slave:
Marie-Lan Nguyen / Wikimedia Commons (Public Domain)

for Ruth

PART ONE

THAT NIGHT AT THE AIRPORT, on the eve of his destruction, Muller climbs to the top of the stairs. He sees a man and woman embracing in a corridor.

'Sebastian?'

His friend looks over, perfectly composed.

'We're here,' Muller says.

'Thanks, man. I'm on my way.'

Sebastian Ashfield has a highbred English accent with a pinch of Australian drawl. It's a charming piece of noise—refined, yet rugged and cool. Think of a cross between an Oxford man and a Marlboro man.

Muller admires him even now, in this startling moment. Sebastian's arms are draped over the woman's shoulders as if he owns her. Her face is buried in his chest. Muller absorbs the scene like a needle injection.

He turns and heads down the stairs. He wanders past travellers and luggage carts, knowing he can't say anything about what he's just witnessed. He doesn't want to cause any trouble. He doesn't want to hurt anybody. Of course, it's not the only reason.

Another man's secret reminds you of your own. That's closer to the truth.

He reaches the waiting area. He sees Sebastian's wife Evelyn and their two children. He sees his own wife Rebekah. They're watching him approach and the lie has already formed in his mind. A simple lie. A bundle of words. He feels the weight of it behind his eyes and notices the moon in the window, swollen almost to fullness, as if about to burst its cold light onto the city.

'Well?' Evelyn says. 'Did you find him?'

Brooding on a secret is like thinking about sex. You don't want people to see the expression on your face. It's best to be alone when you do it.

That night, after returning home, as his wife is falling asleep beside him, Muller unlocks his own secret. He takes it into his hands like a stolen jewel. The yearning fills him, the memories pulse through him in warm colours.

He remembers his first day at the hospital four years earlier.

He's walking down a polished corridor. Dr Margaret Frye is touring him through the facility. She's a middle-aged psychologist, a divorced woman with opinions. She has bright red fingernails, badly chipped, as if she's dipped them in blood and nibbled on them.

Empty wheelchairs are parked along the walls. Through the open doorways of the rooms Muller glimpses his new patients. They're sprawled out on beds and propped up in chairs. They've suffered head injuries and strokes.

Explosions in the brain.

'You need to be hopeful when you're counselling them,' Margaret says quietly. 'Hopeful but realistic. Most of them won't recover. The brain doesn't heal itself.'

'Unlike the heart,' Muller quips.

She gives him a blank look.

Humourless woman, he thinks.

They round a corner and come to the physiotherapy gym, where he sees Lara for the first time. She has an athletic sort of beauty—tanned skin, a high bust, the lean arms of a swimmer.

He doesn't notice her flaw yet.

An old man is next to her, pushing a walker, dragging a leg behind him. 'Lara?' Margaret calls out. 'May I speak with you for a moment?'

Lara comes over and Margaret goes through the introductions. 'Lara, this is Paul Muller, our new psychologist. Paul was at the General for a year—'

'*Muller,*' he says.

'What?'

'I mentioned it earlier. People call me Muller. You know. Nobody calls me Paul.'

'Right. Muller, uh, just transferred. He's going to be with us three days a week.'

'Nice to meet you,' Lara says, with a clever smile that's like a smudge on her lips.

'And you,' he says with a nod.

'Lara is our only physio at the moment,' Margaret continues. 'We usually have two on the unit, but the other position is vacant just now. Lara's been overworked lately.'

'It's not so bad. Keeps me busy.'

'Will you excuse me a minute?' Margaret says, eyeing a woman in a wheelchair. 'I need to check in with Mrs Hendrik about something. I'll be right back.'

As Margaret goes off, Muller nervously glances at Lara and then looks about at the equipment and mirrored walls. He catches a glimpse of his reflection and notices he's slouching. He's always had the posture of a parenthesis.

He straightens up.

'So you're here only three days a week?' Lara says. 'What are you doing on the other two?'

'I'm opening a therapy practice. My own office.'

'Really? Will you have a couch?'

'A couch? I don't think so.'

'But isn't that how it's done—the patient lies on a couch and tells you her dreams?'

He studies her face as he searches for an answer, stumbling on her lips and down her slim brown neck and then clambering back up, over a fierce cheekbone and into her eyes, for he's noticed something that attracts him and yet disturbs him—he can't quite put his finger on it. 'Couches are out of fashion,' he says. 'All you need nowadays are two chairs and a box of tissues.'

Lara smiles. They're staring at each other. It lasts only a second or two, although it's one of those bottomless moments, the kind that new lovers fall into easily, like divers going off a cliff and plunging into the sea.

There's a clatter. The man with the walker is on the floor.

He's fallen, he's moaning. Two assistants are hurrying to his side and Lara dashes over. His mouth is cut and there's blood on his chin as if he's bitten into a small animal.

Margaret returns. 'We should go,' she whispers.

Muller follows her to the door. Lara is squatting beside the old man and Muller steals another look at her, his gaze scuttling down her neck and back to the belt of skin showing around her waist, and she senses him looking and glances over her shoulder.

He sees it, then—her flaw.

It's in the eyes. The left one is smaller. A minor defect, almost imperceptible. She squints as a way of hiding it, giving her an expression of coyness.

Muller sips on the memory of her all morning. He feels like a man who's taken his first drink of water after wandering through a desert—or rather like a man who takes a drink and suddenly realizes how thirsty he is, realizes that his emotional life has been, until now, a barren land.

When he gets back to his office, a little room with a cracked plaster wall, he takes out a sheet of notepaper and writes: 'Love doesn't believe in chance.'

He reads it again. He crosses out the line and writes: 'Love winks an eye at chance.'

It's the start of the poem.

Muller has never published anything in his life, but he fancies himself a poet. In fact, he believes that he might write something good, even great, if only he had the right subject matter—and now he's found it in Lara.

Is he smitten with her? Maybe a little, but it's only a feeling, he tells himself. A sultry breeze of neurochemistry. Besides, he's getting married to Rebekah in a few months and he's never had any doubts about her. Not seriously. They've been together almost two years and he's still fond of her—not in love, but very fond. She's easygoing and pretty, with a glorious horse's mane of hair.

They moved to the coast last autumn and live in an apartment near the downtown. It's a two-story unit, the upper part of a Second Empire house from the late 1800s, with a bay window in the living room where they sit each morning before going to work. They can see the Atlantic Ocean down the road—a patch of grey fuzz, nestled between a convenience store and a junk shop.

'How's your new job?' Rebekah says one day, stroking Yeats the cat.

'People keep asking me what I do on my days off. I tell them I'm starting a therapy practice.'

'You lie?'

'Yes, I lie.'

'Why not tell them the truth?'

'Because the truth, in this case, isn't the sort of thing you tell people.'

'Why not? You told Sebastian and Evelyn.'

'I told them because they don't ask questions. They understand that a writer doesn't want to talk about his writing.'

She opens her hand. 'Look at all this fur.'

'Writing is a private thing.'

'We should brush him more often.'

'The creative process is so delicate. The slightest disturbance and—'

She puts her arm around him. He sighs and leans against her. Flecks of fur waft on the warm air. Snap a shot of that moment—a young couple in a bay window, a fluffy cat purring on the radiator—and you have some idea of their simple happiness, their easy existence.

He takes it for granted, naturally.

Lara gives him signs. She smiles at him in the corridors. She gazes at him a moment too long. He has mixed feelings, of course, about her imperfect eyes, but there are other things about her that are attractive—like the lean fit body, or the olive-brown skin, and then those breasts. They sit way up, like bread buns on a baker's shelf. There's no way to obscure them. They force an element of shamelessness on her personality. He notices that other men give her breasts a second glance, and it seems she's built up a tough outer shell, as if to say, I don't give a damn if you look.

Muller spots her coming out of the nursing station one morning. She's cradling a pile of medical charts. She crosses the corridor and goes into the conference room, nudging the door open with her shoulder.

After some hesitation, Muller walks to the door of the room and sees her through the window. She's alone at the table, opening a binder. The other medical charts are stacked beside her. He can see the names of the patients on their spines. 'Sorry for barging in,' he says, entering. 'I was looking for Ms Kelly's chart.'

'It's your lucky day,' Lara says. 'I've got it right here.'

She takes the binder off the stack and slides it across the table. He notices her fingers and her wedding ring. A gold band with a bright tumour of diamonds. It's a relief knowing that she's married—protects him from any foolish ideas.

He takes the medical chart and sits down across from her. He starts turning pages, nodding to himself, his face growing hot in the silence.

'She's in bad shape, isn't she?' Lara says.

'Ms Kelly? Yes.'

'Do you think she's depressed?'

'More distracted than depressed, I suspect. The stroke knocked out her insight.'

He clicks on his pen and starts writing. The words are small and tight, with nervous spikes, like the tracings of a lie detector.

'So how's your therapy practice going?' she says. 'Have you got that couch yet?'

He looks up from the binder. A thick bar of shutter light lies across her body.

It's a sign. Keep away. No entry.

'I'm taking some time off at the moment,' he says. 'Just relaxing. You know? A little reading. A little writing.'

'That's interesting. What kind of writing?'

'It's nothing serious. I only dabble. Actually, I'm working on a poem right now.'

'What's it about?'

'I usually don't talk about my writing. I don't even tell my fiancée—Rebekah. Not while the work is in progress.

But if you really want to know—to put it generally—the poem is about beauty. People say that we can't explain God, but I believe that beauty is more complicated than God. More difficult to fathom.'

'I'm not sure I'm following you.'

'Think of it this way. Beauty, like God, is transcendent, and yet we see it every day. Sometimes we see it right in front of us. We feel its power, and its mystique, and yet—and this is the thing—what happens when we try to describe it?'

She leans forward, squishing her bosom against the table's edge. 'What happens?'

'We, uh. Diminish it.'

'I still don't get it,' she says, squinting with perplexity.

'What I'm saying is, beauty, true beauty, overwhelms us with its dazzling light. It leaves us at a loss for words—so much so that we can only fail when we try to articulate it. Poetry is the best we can do when speaking of beauty. The least of all insults, you might say. Therefore the highest form of praise.'

'Wow. That's pretty deep.'

'I'm sorry, I don't mean to be so abstract. The poem itself is quite tangible.'

'Tangible?'

'Capable of being. You know. Grasped.'

There's screeching outside.

A pair of gulls in the loading bay. They're fighting over a crust of pizza.

'Tell me a few lines,' she says. 'Come on.'

'Of the poem? No. Not while it's in progress.'

'But why?' she laughs. 'What's the worst that could happen?'

'I could lose it.'

'Lose the poem? How would you *lose* it?'

'I could lose the feel of it. It could slip away. Silently. Invisibly.'

She sits back, watching him with her imperfect eyes, and presses her pen against her lips. 'You're different, you know. In a nice way.'

Maybe that's why she likes him? Because he's different. Because of the way he speaks. He folds words and ideas like origami.

She's one-quarter Punjabi, she tells him. Her grandfather, a British officer, married an Indian girl (she jokes that she got good skin from the deal, and loves cooking with curry). She confesses that she doesn't read books, only magazines. She's a long-distance runner and placed fourth in last year's coastal marathon. She lives in West Abbey, a small town a few kilometres from the city, and mentions her husband, Dimitri, as incidentally as he mentions Rebekah— as if they're trivial fixtures in their lives. Like kitchen tables and armchairs.

He knows what's happening. They're feeling out the boundaries. *Flirting* is the proper term. Nor does it matter that they don't have much in common. Chalk and cheese, as they say—or is it chalk and chutney in this case? The conversation only ends when a nurse comes into the room for a medical chart.

Muller leaves feeling guilty, but thrilled. His heart thuds like a gavel and he spends the day thinking about Lara, jotting bits of verse between appointments.

That night he watches Rebekah over the rim of a book. She's on her hands and knees, arching her back.

'My mother would kill me if she saw me doing this,' she says.

'Sticking your bum in the air?'

'Doing yoga.'

'Why? Because it's unchristian?'

Rebekah's mother lives in Toronto. She's a gentle woman who grimaces when she smiles, as if it pains her. She mails them postcards with pictures of bouquets and sunbeams breaking through clouds, always with Bible quotations on the back.

'She asked me about the wedding,' Rebekah says. 'Asked me to reconsider. About the church.'

'What did you tell her?'

'I told her we'd think about it.'

'I'm not getting married in a church, Bek.'

'I wasn't sure how to let her down. I'll tell her another time.'

'You'd better. Because I'm not—'

'*I know.* I'll tell her, okay?'

She arches her back. Her bum, he notices, is shaped like an overripe fig. With a pang of disappointment he admits it again—he's not in love with her anymore. That doesn't mean he doesn't like her, or isn't comfortable with her, or doesn't want to marry her. He's simply not in love. The surge of desire that brought them together in the beginning, that intoxicating emotion, that sweet elixir of hormones—it faded long ago.

Maybe he ought to end the relationship?

No. That would be a mistake. Because Muller understands something deeper: sooner or later he'd feel the same way about any other woman. Even Lara. He's sure of it. Love never lasts. Love is like a suntan—it either burns you or it fades away. Every man knows this. Not every woman does, but the men all do. What then is the point of leaving one woman for another? Why bother when the end result will be the same?

So he won't leave Rebekah. But he can't give up Lara either. The feeling is too strong—at least for the moment.

He makes small talk with her in the nursing station and the corridors of the hospital. He impresses her with words like *soporific* and *vertiginous*. He makes up jokes for her amusement: 'What do you call a depressed cantaloupe? *Melon*-choly.'

It's all so innocent.

Late one afternoon, near Christmas, he pauses at the door of the physio gym.

She's alone in the back office.

'You're still here?' he calls out.

'Oh hi,' she says. 'Come on in.'

He crosses through the darkened gym, knees wobbly. Her office is a cramped, windowless space with four cubicles.

A wedding photo is propped by the phone. Lara is

laughing into the camera and Dimitri is grinning with a dab of cake on his nose. His head is like a football helmet—large and bald, with a projecting jaw.

'I was about to leave,' she says. 'I'm starting my holidays tomorrow.'

'I guess I won't see you for a couple of weeks.'

She brushes some paper-clips into a drawer. 'I guess not. Doing anything special for Christmas?'

'Special? No. We'll be here—in town—just sort of. You know. I'll work on my writing. My poem.'

'The beauty poem? You're still working on that?'

'It's a labour of love.'

'Maybe you'll show it to me one day.'

'Maybe. When it's done.'

'Is that a promise?'

'Well, I suppose.'

She gets up and softly jabs him in the chest with a finger. 'Then I expect you to keep it.'

He catches a whiff of her breath—peppermint gum. Almost kills him. She takes her coat off a hook. 'Why did you become a psychologist anyway? If you like writing so much?'

'My father convinced me it wasn't practical to be a writer. So I got a profession.'

'Now you're a real doctor. Made papa proud, I guess?'

'Actually, I'm not a *real* doctor.'

'What do you mean?'

'I don't inject people with needles. Just words.'

'Do you ever stop quapping?'

'*Quipping*,' he says. 'Unless you meant a combination of quipping and quacking?'

She smiles, buttoning her coat. 'Do you have any new vocabulary for me? Something I can remember for the holiday?'

'How about *gestalt*?'

'Meaning?'

'A whole that's greater than the sum of its parts.'

'Gestalt. That's nice.'

'It's a German word. Not many nice German words.'

'Do you speak German too?'

'I used to study it, but I gave up. Speaking German is like wearing a straitjacket on your tongue.'

'Funny boy.' She takes out her gloves and moulds them in her hands. 'Anyway, I guess this is goodbye.'

'Yeah, I guess.'

There's a moment, then, that he won't remember. He'll never know who moved forward first. All he'll ever know—all he knows now—is that they're hugging. A warm body-to-body embrace. The most important things in life happen when we're not looking.

'Wait,' she whispers.

She pushes the door shut. She slips her arms around him again and sighs. Her face is pressed against his chest, and his is bowed on her shoulder, and everything vanishes— walls, cubicles, obligations, wedding plans. They fall away like flower petals.

'I'm going to miss you,' she whispers.

'I'll miss you too.'

They look at each other and a flicker of restlessness goes through him. It occurs to him that no matter what happens next, no matter how far things go, it won't get any better than this—gazing into Lara's eyes. They're beautiful just now.

There's a knock at the door.

'Lara?' comes a gruff voice. 'Are you in there?'

It's Dimitri. She greets him with a noisy smooch and makes apologies while Muller crouches behind the door, his nose pressed against an exercise ball.

The office goes dark.

Their voices fade into the corridor. Dimitri's cologne lingers in the air—an aggressive metallic scent, like a crowbar smeared in aftershave.

Muller waits a minute and then hurries to the patient lounge. The windows overlook the front entrance of the building. Lara and Dimitri are getting into a pickup truck. The headlights come on and glower at him. They say, Stay away from my wife. They say, Don't even think about it, buddy. Flurries are spinning in the air and the vehicle pulls away and Muller feels a sharp tug in his heart, like a fish getting yanked out of water.

He spends the next two weeks in a whirlpool of longing. He can't get her out of his head. He starts cooking meals with curry. He goes jogging despite his bad knees. He eats artichokes because she's a firm believer in antioxidants.

Muller knows he's obsessed. Of course, he's guilty too. How can he get involved with a woman when he's about to marry Rebekah? Is he bored? Is he looking for an escape?

All he knows for sure is that he's fumbling along, getting swept up in his feelings, and that's his mistake. His fatal error. Really, if there's anything Muller is going to learn about having an affair, it's this: you must never, never fumble through it. You need to plan. You need to think rationally. You must be prepared to hide things and to lie to the people who trust you. You need to behave as if everything is okay—and it's all the more difficult because you must not only deceive others, but also yourself. The mask of deception faces both directions, inside and out.

He'll learn, too, that even if you can do all of those things, there are no guarantees, and there never can be in affairs. But if you choose to fumble along, thinking you won't make a mistake—well, that's inviting disaster.

In Muller's case, it happens one night at the Ashfields' house.

Sebastian and Evelyn Ashfield: they're Muller and Rebekah's best friends in town. Their only friends, really. An English couple. They're civilized but not too pretentious, like minor royalty. Not a prince and princess, but a lord and his lady. They moved here about a year ago, around the same time as Muller and Rebekah, and claimed that they left England because it was becoming too crowded. They wanted to raise their children in a more spacious and peaceful place.

Evelyn is the daughter of an Anglican minister. She turned out an atheist, but Muller senses in her character the calm and orderliness of a church liturgy, and some judgement too, as if the very thing she rejected is cemented into her bones.

Sebastian, who happens to be an atheist too, has a different kind of presence, more like a cathedral—imposing and strong and prone to deep silence. He grew up in Australia but never says much about his past, and Muller and Rebekah never pry, not wanting to seem impolite.

The Ashfields live downtown in a quaint green row house, where they regularly invite Muller and Rebekah for supper. That night, the night of Muller's blunder, the couples line their chairs by the living room window after the meal. Sitting in a row, facing the glass panes, they gaze across the lights of town toward the blackness of the Atlantic.

'Did you hear about the bananas?' Rebekah says.

'The bananas?' Evelyn says.

'I heard they're going extinct.'

'Might you be confusing bananas with Bengal tigers?' Muller says. 'The resemblance, after all.'

'I heard it in the news, just the other day. Seriously. In ten years there won't be any more bananas left in the world.'

'You're quite right, Rebekah,' Sebastian says. 'I read the same story in the *Telegraph*. It's because bananas are sterile. They're all descended from the same plant.'

'An original Adam banana?' Muller says.

'Yes, indeed.'

'Be fruitful and multiply, saith the Lord.'

Sebastian passes out the cigar box. They puff on Café Crèmes. 'Oh, I forgot to mention,' Rebekah says. 'We've decided on a venue for the wedding. It'll be a chapel at the University of Toronto.'

'It's not strictly a chapel,' Muller says. 'It doubles as a classroom. There won't be a minister.'

'Barney *is* technically a minister.'

'He is, but he's Unitarian.'

'What does that mean?' Evelyn says.

'It means he believes whatever you believe,' Muller says. 'He believes in everything. Or nothing. Whichever you prefer. We found him on the Internet.'

'I suppose that simplifies things.'

'It sure does. Marriage is just a click away.'

'I forgot to mention, we should order the invitations this week,' Rebekah says.

A cloud of weariness passes over his face. 'Weddings can be stressful,' Evelyn says, catching his reflection in the window.

'We're managing well enough,' he says. 'And it'll be nice to finally. You know. Settle down.'

Rebekah looks at him.

'I meant it in the positive sense.'

She squashes her cigarillo in the ashtray. The children, Kate and David, are asleep in their bedroom, and Muller can hear their breathing through a monitor beside Evelyn. A sound like distant tides.

He clears his throat. 'All I meant is, there's an adjustment. I think we can both agree that there's an adjustment?'

'I don't find it difficult.'

'Marriage *is* an adjustment, Bek, isn't it? And I strongly

suspect—correct me if I'm wrong, Sebastian—I suspect it's more of a challenge for the man than for the woman.' He waits. Sebastian says nothing. Muller shifts in his chair and continues: 'What I mean is, a man is like a hunter. You know? A hunter. He spends years roaming through the dating wilderness, searching for the right woman, and then he finds her, he captures her in his net, so to speak—and then he suddenly realizes he has to put away his net. He has to give up the game—which is fine. It's perfectly fine, but it's an adjustment. You see? A change. I mean, what was it like for you, Sebastian?'

'Change can certainly bring a sense of loss.'

'Exactly! *Loss*. Loss is what I'm talking about.'

Rebekah picks at a fingernail. He hears the children's breathing. Moths of snow are fluttering through the harbour lights.

'Anyone for a glass of port?' Sebastian says.

'Yes,' Evelyn says. 'Port would be wonderful.'

So there it is. His blunder. Muller doesn't often say monumentally stupid things—he's too conscious of language, too careful with words—but as the four friends sip their port and munch on cashews, he realizes that he was the victim of his own conscience. His guilt about Lara. He needed to confess something, it seems—a little something—to ease the pressure.

Muller and Rebekah walk home that night. Their apartment is only ten minutes away. Snowflakes are still falling, gently smashing into their faces.

'Bek,' Muller says. 'I'm sorry about what I said earlier. It didn't come out right. I'm glad that we're together. I'm glad we're getting married. Are you okay?'

'I'm fine.'

He takes her mitted hand. He gives it a squeeze and she squeezes back but says nothing.

It's relationship Morse code: Let's drop the subject.

The next day he goes for a walk through town. The roads are slathered in slush, and a crack in his heel gulps water with each step. The stores are open and the post-Christmas sales are in full swing. Rags of tinsel dangle from the lampposts. Garbage bags are piled on the curbs between grimy heaps of snow. How seedy it always looks, the remains of the holiday. Like seeing an actor after a performance, just when the make-up is getting smeared off.

He passes a café, The Tin Cup. He spots Rebekah inside, from behind—the familiar mass of golden hair. She's at a table with the Ashfields. She was at home when he left over an hour earlier. Sebastian is speaking to her. Evelyn is listening with Kate on her knee, and David is picking at a muffin.

Under any other circumstance Muller would gladly join them, but instead he keeps walking. He's been thinking about Lara all afternoon, fervently yearning for her, and he can't imagine anything more wonderful just now than to prolong this nebulous feeling.

It's dark when he gets back to the apartment. He puts a log in the fireplace. He settles onto the couch with a plate of butter cookies and a book by Rilke—*Letters to a Young Poet*. A certain line speaks to him, and he reads it over and over: 'Have patience with everything unresolved in your heart and try to love the questions themselves...'

How true, how right! Beneath all his longing, Muller has been agonizing about what will happen between him and Lara—but now, gazing off at the fire while clutching the book prayerfully under his chin, he realizes that rather than struggling against his uncertainty he ought to welcome that great question mark. The hook that pierces his chest.

He closes his eyes and recalls the hug in her office. The sense of melting into her. Oh, he must be grateful for this, this sweet anguish, he must accept the contradiction—*embrace* the contradiction!—that he'll be marrying one woman when he's fallen for another.

Fallen in *love*?

He hears the front door. Footsteps on the lower stairway. He sits up and props a pillow behind him. Rebekah comes into the room with a grocery bag. 'Oh hello,' he says. 'I was wondering where you'd gone.'

'I was at Sebastian and Evelyn's. I meant to call.'

Yeats leaps off the radiator and brushes against her ankle. Muller holds up the book. 'I've been reading Rilke. It's incredible. Profound. You *must* read this.'

'I brought home some pasta sauce for you.' She takes a plastic container out of the bag. 'Have you had any supper yet?'

'I'm not hungry. But this book—really.'

She sits on the edge of the coffee table. 'Where did you go?'

'Here and there. How are Sebastian and Evelyn?'

'They're good. We talked about some things, actually.'

'About what things?'

'What you said last night.'

'What I said?'

'About the man being a hunter and all that.'

'You talked about *that*? God, Bek. You know I hate it when you get into our private business with other people.'

'I didn't think it was private.'

'Exactly what did you tell them?'

'I told them I was hurt by what you said.'

'Why didn't you tell *me*?'

'I thought you already knew.'

'I did know, and I thought you were over it. Didn't we talk about it when we walked home?'

'Yes, but—'

'Did you get into our intimate life?'

'What are you talking about? It wasn't anything like that.'

'So what did you tell them?'

'I just told you—that I was hurt. That it made me wonder, you know, if you were really serious about the wedding.'

'I *am* serious. How the hell could you doubt that?'

'Well, because—'

'And what did they say?'

'They mostly listened. Sebastian said he'd be open to talking with you. If you were interested.'

'Sebastian wants to talk with *me*?'

'As a friend.'

'Well, well. How noble of him.' Muller shakes his head

in disgust. 'I don't have any doubts about getting married, alright? Either you trust me or you don't. God, I can't believe you got into our private business. You ought to know better, Bek.'

'Is there somebody else?'

'What?'

'Is there a woman?'

'Bek, Bek, Bek. What kind of question is that?'

'You're preoccupied.'

'Is *that* what you talked about with them?'

'You're not sure about the wedding.'

'Is *that* what you said to them?'

'*No*. I just said you're not sure—'

'I *am* sure. How many times do I—!'

'Don't shout!'

'I'm shouting because you're not listening!'

They glare at each other. She gets up and storms off, stumbling over Yeats. The container flies out of her hands and splatters against the wall. She hurries away in tears. Tomato sauce is running down the panels like somebody got shot.

He climbs up the stairs. The upper floor is dark. She's curled on the bed.

He enters the room and stands over her with a mask of streetlight against his face. 'I'm sorry, Bek. I shouldn't have shouted.'

She stares toward the window. He sits down on the corner of the mattress. 'Bek.'

'What.'

'I do want to get married. I want us to be together. I wish you would believe that.'

He watches her in the dim light. A teardrop hangs from her lashes like a glass ornament. 'Where did you go this afternoon,' she says.

'I walked around town. I collected images for my writing. It's the truth—I can show you my notes if you don't believe me. As for last night, I don't know why I said those things. I didn't mean it the way you heard it. I've been stressed lately.'

'Why are you stressed?'

'My writing's stalled. You know what that does to me. When my writing isn't going well.'

Yeats leaps onto the bed. He curls up against Rebekah's belly. She starts stroking him and looks at Muller. 'What are you writing?'

'A poem.'

'What kind of poem?'

He laughs. 'It's just a poem. I thought we were talking about the wedding? And I *don't* have any doubts, Bek. I *do* want to get married. Really.'

He crawls onto the bed. He puts his arms around her. There's no need to recount all the details of what he says to reassure her—the soothing promises, the half lies, the ten-percent truths. In the end she believes him, and Muller is convinced too. He wants to spend his life with her. It doesn't matter that his passion, that frothy little river, is being channelled toward another woman. Marriage isn't built on passion.

New Year's comes and goes. There's a staff meeting on his first day back at work. Lara is startling under the cool gleam of the tube lights. He almost forgot how lovely she is, how beguiling. He doesn't even notice the difference in her eyes. Two weeks of yearning have airbrushed away her imperfections.

He follows her to the lobby during the break. She sits by the elevators with a juice bottle in her lap.

Muller walks up. They gaze at each other. 'I missed you,' she says.

'I—I missed you too.'

'I remembered the word you gave me.'

'Gestalt?'

'A whole that's bigger than the parts. Like us.'

A spear of warmth impales him. He smiles dumbly.

'Why don't you have a seat?' she says.

'It might look suspicious.'

'We could be talking about patients.'

'Did your husband say anything? After he came up to the gym. When we were. You know.'

'Everything's fine. Don't worry. Did you have a nice holiday?'

He glances over his shoulder. A couple of nurses are chatting by the water fountain.

'Are you okay?' she says.

'There are so many people around.'

'You're sort of the nervous type, aren't you?'

'I'm neurotic, I suppose.'

'Neurotic?'

'It's like being anxious and inhibited at the same time. Like a can of Coke that's been shaken and shaken but never opened.'

She laughs. 'I don't drink Coke.'

'I just meant, you know—I don't know what I meant. Listen, are you free at lunch? I could give you a call.'

'Why don't we meet instead? You have your own office, right?'

'It would be too risky. People are always coming and going in the hallway. But I'd love to meet. Yes.'

She sucks on her straw with a smile. 'I think I know another place,' she says. 'But I'll have to double-check. Can I call you a little later?'

After the staff meeting, Muller makes a hurried visit to the in-patient unit. He schedules a few appointments for later in the day, and then returns to his office and remains there for the rest of the morning, close to his phone, quivering with excitement. She *missed* him! She knows a *place* where they can meet! He's too thrilled to reflect on the consequences of what might happen next. He can't think clearly at all. He tries to do some paperwork. He tries to work on the poem but feels like a man composing music in a tornado.

Lara calls him at noon. 'We're all set,' she says. 'Are you free?'

'Yes,' he says, trembling. 'I have a bit of time.' He starts scouring his drawer for a pack of breath mints while she gives him directions.

He leaves his office and takes the north elevator to the

basement. It opens onto a cement corridor. The air is warm and stuffy, and pipes stretch along the ceiling. He passes lockers and a maintenance area. He comes to an intersection and turns left.

There's a series of doors, green and windowless. He stops at the third one, just as she instructed, and after a glance up and down the corridor gives a couple of quick knocks.

The door opens a crack.

'Come in,' she whispers.

He slips inside and beholds it: their meeting place, their holy of holies. An old storage room, twenty by twenty feet, with a small ground-floor window stained with dust and snow. Physiotherapy equipment was kept here at one time and she still has a key. Prosthetic limbs hang from the ceiling now. Plastic arms and legs. They look like slabs of meat, or stalactites, and soon he and Lara will be joking about whether to call the place 'the cave' or 'the butchery'.

They meet during lunch on most Mondays, Tuesdays, and Wednesdays—the days that Muller is at work. Their relationship isn't complicated. They hug standing up. They sway with their eyes closed. They whisper sweet and flattering things to each other.

You're beautiful.

It's so good to hold you.

You feel like home.

It's innocent as affairs go, and that's how he wants to keep it. In fact, he has rules about what they can and can't do. He doesn't know how he came up with these rules—they simply appeared in his mind, right from the start. He never talks about the rules with Lara, although she seems to understand them and to follow them, albeit with a mild air of disappointment.

There's no kissing allowed. There's no groping under the clothes, and no fondling of the breasts or crotch. Thrusting their hips gently while hugging is okay, but only for a few seconds. Dirty talk isn't permitted, and they can't use the word 'love' either.

It's all about restraint. Maybe you find that hard to believe—a man resisting his passions? But Muller is reluctant to give up control of himself. The wedding date is looming and he, a naturally timid creature, prefers to be cautious, content with what he has, like a boy with a big lollipop who decides to hold the lollipop rather than to lick it, knowing that it can't vanish or give him a cavity as long as he never puts it in his mouth.

They sit on the floor one day. She lays her head on his lap, gazing up at him while he strokes her hair.

He studies the difference in her eyes and wonders if she was born that way. He wonders if it could be surgically corrected.

'What's the matter?' she says.

'Nothing.'

'What were you thinking?'

'I was thinking—about Iraq.'

'Iraq?'

'Whether there's going to be a war. A random thought.'

'Saddam Hussein is a monster.'

'What if it's American propaganda?'

'He's better off dead.' She tugs his hand. 'Come lie on top of me.'

'I think we should stand.'

'Fine, we'll stand.'

They get up and wrap their arms around each other. She clutches his skinny buttocks. She massages them and rubs her pelvis against him. 'Do you have fantasies about me?' she whispers in his ear.

'Yes.'

'Do you think about me when you're with Rebekah?'

'Yes.'

'What do you think about?'

'I imagine that she's you.'

'How?'

'What do you mean, *how*?'

'I mean how do you do it?'

'I narrow my eyes. I make them blurry and imagine that her legs are yours. I imagine her arms are yours.'

'Is that nice—imagining me where I shouldn't be?' she says, grinning against his ear.

She slips her fingers behind his belt. He grabs her wrist. 'No,' he says. 'We can't.'

'Why not?'

'Lara, please.'

'But I don't get it. If we can fantasize about each other, if we can do all these things in our heads, then why can't we do the same things in real life?'

'We can't get carried away. One thing leads to another.'

'Isn't that the way it's supposed to happen?'

'We don't want to hurt anybody. I don't want to hurt Rebekah. You don't want to hurt Dimitri. And the other thing is—'

'What other thing?'

'I don't want to use up our feelings in the physical act. Our feelings are preserved when we don't act on them.'

'Don't you think our feelings would get *stronger* if we acted on them?'

'No—I mean, think about it. If we acted on our feelings, we'd lose the sense of mystery. The sense of not fully knowing each other. I want to preserve that.'

'I'm not a jar of marmalade. I don't want to be preserved.' She lets go of him.

'Lara, come on.'

'You hardly ever touch me,' she says sharply.

'What? I hug you, don't I?'

'And it's not even about touching. It's your whole attitude. It's like you're afraid of me.'

'I know this is a bit complicated.'

'It's complicated because you *make* it complicated.' She turns away and swats a prosthetic arm that's hanging before her. It swings on its hook, squealing meekly.

'Listen,' he says. 'I do want to be close to you—and I *do* want to touch you. Of course! It's just, you know, the situation.'

Light is filtering through the window, flashing against the swinging limb. Lara reaches up and unhooks it. 'Let's say you could touch me. With this.'

'Touch you with *that*?'

'That way you're not actually touching me. Here.'

She pushes the prosthetic into his hands. It's stiff and cold and ham-coloured. He holds it by the elbow, mildly repulsed.

'What am I supposed to do?'

'*Touch* me.'

'You really want me to do this?'

'Yes. We can try something simple. Like this.'

She moves closer, and takes the fingers of the prosthetic. She touches them to her breast. The gesture has a strange solemnity about it, as if she's about to take an oath. She glances at him with a warm smile, and begins to trace the stiff fingers in a slow, sensuous circle. Muller feels like a boy peeking through the window of a strip club. Her shirt is nylon, skin-tight, and the fingertips make a soft depression as she guides them across her well-sculpted bosom.

He tightens his hold around the end of the prosthetic. She lets go of it, and he shifts his grip down, taking over the full weight of the limb, and begins moving it on his own. She narrows her eyes and drapes her arms around her head. Take me. Ravish me. He paws her boob with slow cautious strokes. He can feel her contours through the artificial fingers the way a blind man using a stick feels the road through the tip of the stick. He's *touching* her, *feeling* her, but he *isn't*. What a miracle, this touching-but-not-touching, this gorgeous contradiction—and suddenly it's gone. He becomes aware of his hands around the prosthetic. The grip of his own fingers around the hard plastic. He becomes aware of himself and his guilt that only moments earlier was just a fire in the distance, a glow on the horizon of consciousness. It's all around him now. He's burning in guilt and needs to escape, needs to find his way back to the feeling of her body.

Lara gives a murmuring exhalation. The sound has a jostling effect. He looks at the fingers of the prosthetic. Their tips come alive again. They're brushing her. He's recovered the warmth and softness of those immaculate buns of flesh. There's bellowing in the corridor. The hospital loudspeaker. 'Doctor Paul Muller, please return to your office. Doctor Paul Muller.'

'Oh God,' he says.

'What is it?'

'I have an early appointment. I forgot. Can we, uh, continue another time?'

She sighs.

'I'm sorry, Lara.'

'Just go.'

He puts down the prosthetic. He leaves the room and starts running down the corridor, hopping a few times while tugging at his crotch to adjust his erection. He dashes three floors up a stairwell and finds his patient, a young man in a hoody, waiting in a wheelchair by the office door.

'My apologies, Tim,' Muller says.

'Is it the right day?' his patient asks.

Muller unlocks the door, panting. 'You got it right, Tim. I was held up in a meeting.'

'I asked the lady to call you.'

'The lady?'

'I wasn't sure it was the right day. Is it Tuesday?'

'It is, yes. Now where would you like to begin? How is your rehab going this week?'

He muddles through the session, distracted and throbbing with the memory of how he touched her. It isn't the first time that he can't focus on his work because of Lara, although his patients never seem to notice. Most of them, like Tim, have brain injuries that diminish their concentration and memory. Their mental lives are already clouded, camouflaging Muller's negligence.

After a half hour, vaguely ashamed, he wheels the young man back to his room. He wanders into the nursing station on the chance that Lara might be checking her mail. There's a memo in his box—something about a committee. He slips it into the recycling bin and decides to call her. He needs to apologize again for running off.

He starts back to his office, tantalized at the thought of touching her again. Maybe tomorrow?

The door across from his office is open. Margaret Frye looks up from her desk: 'Paul, can I see you for a minute?'

He walks over.

'Close the door if you would,' she says. 'Have a seat.'

He senses something is amiss. She isn't looking at him. He takes the chair across from her. 'How was your session with Tim?' she says, rustling some papers together.

'It went well. Very well.'

'He was waiting for you in his room.'

'I know,' Muller chuckles. 'I marked the wrong time in

my agenda by accident. One thirty instead of twelve thirty.'

She pushes the glasses over the bump of her nose. 'I wanted to ask you something, Paul. Have you been spending time with Lara?'

'Lara?' he says with a gulp. 'Oh, I suppose we chat on occasion, if that's what you mean.'

'Some of the staff have noticed that the two of you chat quite a bit.'

'Quite a bit?'

'It doesn't look good, Paul.'

'We're only talking.'

'May I suggest, then, that you have your *tête-à-tête*'s on your own time?'

'We talk about *work*, Margaret. About our patients. There's nothing wrong with talking to a colleague.'

'No, there isn't. But based on what others have been saying, it seems that your conversations with Lara are—I mean, appear—excessive.'

'Others? What others?'

'It doesn't matter.'

'And define *excessive*, please.'

'I'm not here to quibble with you.'

'Is four minutes excessive? Six?'

'It's the appearance, Paul. The optics. It doesn't matter to me what the facts are.'

'If you want to accuse me of something, then say it.'

'I'm not accusing you. I'm raising a concern.'

He mashes his finger against the desktop. 'The facts are this. We are colleagues. We talk about patients. We talk in the nursing station and the conference room, just like anybody else.'

'I hear it's not the only place.'

He grips the armrest, bracing himself. 'What, are you spying on me now?'

'Nobody is spying. One of the nursing staff saw you and Lara in the lobby one night. By the vending machines.'

'One night?' he laughs. 'It was after five o'clock. I was on my way out the door when I saw her getting a bottle of juice. I stopped and we chatted for a minute. God, this is absurd! You ought to know better, Margaret. The nursing staff are gossips. Every one of them.'

'It's not only the nursing staff.'

'Oh please! Is this a witch hunt? Aren't men and women allowed to talk without everybody assuming the worst? This is utterly absurd! You are accusing me—'

'I'm not accusing you, Paul.'

'You are *insinuating* that I'm having a relationship with this woman, just before my wedding, and in full view of the entire hospital. Do you think I'm a fool? Do you think I would actually do that? Do you really believe that?'

She watches him steadily.

'And by the way, people call me Muller,' he says, getting to his feet. 'Not Paul. *Muller! Muller!*'

He's amazed at his performance. What magnificent outrage! He walks out of the room shaking his head, his eyes screwed up at the heavens.

'Unbelievable,' he mutters. 'Just unbelievable.'

He crosses the hall to his office and closes the door. He slumps into his chair. Lays his head on the desk. His temple pulses feverishly.

You thought you could get away with this. You're an idiot. A colossal bloody idiot.

He phones Lara and tells her everything. 'You need to calm down,' she says in a low voice. 'It's not that bad.'

'What do you mean not that bad? There are suspicions. Rumours.'

'But it doesn't sound like anybody really *knows* anything.'

'So what? *Rumours*, Lara, *rumours*! They're like—'

'Calm down.'

'—they're like frogs.'

'Frogs?'

'Like disgusting little frogs, leaping out of people's mouths and into other people's ears.'

She's laughing.

'It's not funny.'

'Muller, listen. It's all just talk. She doesn't even know about the room.'

'What if someone *else* knows? What if someone's watching us? What about that window in the corner of the room?'

'Come on, Muller, there's always rumours in the hospital.'

'We need to be careful. I think we should cool things off—temporarily.'

'Cool things off?'

'Until the dust settles.'

'Meaning what exactly?'

'I mean, I don't think we should meet for a while. We can't be seen chatting.'

'You're getting married next week anyway,' she says glumly.

'That's got nothing to do with it.'

'No?'

'Please, Lara. We just need to let the dust settle.'

A bar clangs in the physio gym. 'I feel like I'm always waiting for you,' she whispers.

'Waiting for me? Lara, people are *talking* about us. We can't have rumours flying all over the place. It'll only be for a while, and then—'

'How long is a while?'

'Until I get back. Then we can see each other again. Then we can figure something out.'

He hears another clang. Faint laughter. 'Do you care about me?' she says.

'What?'

'You heard me.'

'Of course I care about you.'

'Then call me from Toronto.'

'You want me to call you from Toronto?'

'Yes. On your wedding day.'

'Are you crazy?'

'You call me, Muller, or it's over.'

'Are you trying to torture me?'

'I want to know if you're serious. If you're serious then you'll do it—a simple call to my office.'

'I can call you on any other day, but *not* on that day.'

'No. It has to be the wedding day. It'll be a Saturday, right? You can leave a message if I'm not here—although you never know. I might be. I have some paperwork to catch up on.'

'For God's sake, do you have any idea how *busy* a wedding day is?'

'I'm married, in case you forgot.'

'What is that supposed to mean?'

'It means I know what I'm asking you to do.'

'Lara *please*. Why are you making this more difficult?'

'A simple call. That's all I want.'

'I can't do it. I don't even have a cell phone! How am I supposed to reach you?'

'Toronto's a big city. Find a pay phone. You've got my number.'

Someone once said the only thing constant in life is change. That may be true, even obvious, but it doesn't make it any less painful. Change can crush us slowly, inch by inch, like the pressure of a moving glacier, or it can sweep us away quickly, like a flash flood. We can fight against these kinds of change, even if it's hopeless. We can try to push back on the glacier or swim against the current. That's what Muller thinks he's dealing with—change that you can see and to a small degree resist. But there's a third kind of change, which is the worst and most devious kind, the invisible sort that burrows under the earth, digging a hole right under your feet. It's already finished before you know it.

Muller is standing over just such a hole, and it's deeper than he could have imagined, reaching far into the future. The ground hasn't collapsed beneath him yet, although he has a dim sense that one day it will, and that he'll fall, and Rebekah will fall with him, tumbling toward some catastrophe.

They fly to Toronto and spend a few days on the final wedding preparations. He walks down the aisle with a phoney grin on his face. Fifty-nine guests watch him and snap pictures while the guilt squirms in him like a worm. He wishes, now, that he never got involved with Lara. He wants the affair to be over—and he decides that it is.

Now.

It's finished.

Not that he's convinced. He's made the same decision many times over the past week, never fully believing it. But it comforts him to make the decision, at least for the moment—and he knows that with enough of these moments, these lies, stretched out like stepping stones, he can cross whole rivers of anguish, whole lakes of guilt and fire.

He's in survival mode—doing what you have to do, believing what you have to believe.

He reaches the altar. Barney, the minister, is a beanpole of a man in a black frock. The fabric is thin and the colours of a Hawaiian shirt are showing through. He watches Muller with keen, sparkling eyes. They met him for the first time a couple of days ago. 'So tell me why you want to get married?' he'd asked. The question was so direct that even Rebekah was thrown off. They laughed and fumbled to answer, sipping from cups of liquorice tea.

Muller can't bear the man and looks toward the windows. A squirrel is clattering on an ivy wall. Sparrows flash over the building. He notices a lone cloud, wispy and high—he forgot how high the sky is here, so far from the sea—and wonders if the Ashfields might still show up.

They sent an apologetic email last night. Planes have been grounded because of heavy fog. It's like a blanket on the coast and shows no signs of moving. They probably won't make it.

Their absence is a consolation. He feels less pressure. The string trio starts into 'Jesu, Joy of Man's Desiring'. Rebekah's mother comes out of a room at the back of the chapel, and Rebekah emerges a moment later in a strapless white gown, her long curled hair draped extravagantly over her shoulders.

Whispers of awe flutter about the room. The two women start up the aisle arm in arm. There's a shower of clicks and flashes. He wonders if the Ashfields might have heard any rumours? Is that why they haven't come? Sebastian works at the General, Evelyn at the Psychiatric Institute. They might have caught something through the grapevine.

He's being paranoid. Needs to relax. *Relax*, for God's sake! Rebekah turns to him at the altar and he pulls up his sagging smile.

The music goes silent.

Barney sweeps his bright gaze back and forth across the guests like a searchlight, and then he looks at Rebekah, and then at Muller, and then down at his paper with a satisfied nod, and at last he begins to speak.

As his nasally voice fills up the stone room, Muller is determined to maintain the appearance of composure. He keeps his chin up and his shoulders back, listening with a smile as hot bolts of anxiety shoot up through his neck and into his face. He does everything they rehearsed with pains-taking care––stepping forward, touching his candle to the flame, stepping back, repeating vows—while on the inside, deep down, he's hunkered in his bomb shelter, waiting for the explosions of guilt to end.

He's got a pounding headache by the time the ceremony is over. The reception is next door at Victoria College. After supper and the speeches he and Rebekah lead the first dance in the lobby. The music makes him misty-eyed. He sniffles and nuzzles her nose in the dimmed light. They exchange a kiss to the whooping of the onlookers.

The dancing fizzles out after a few songs and every-body meanders back into the dining hall. He gets trapped in a conversation with his father and Rebekah's mother. His father talks slowly as if his thoughts are precious gifts that must be opened carefully: 'I knew Paul. Was a special boy. When he looked out of the car. And he saw the moon. And the lampposts. And the lampposts. Were passing. Quickly. And he wondered. Why? They moved? But the moon? Stayed? Still?'

He spots Rebekah with her friends. She's so beautiful when she laughs.

He can't believe he betrayed her. He can't believe he's

got a long-distance calling card in his pocket. There's a pay phone in the basement.

The pounding in his head thickens. A vein in his temple is pulsing like a caterpillar.

'He was always. A smart. Boy.'

'Dad,' he says. 'Come on.'

'A doctor.'

'I'm not a real doctor.'

'You're a *fine* young man,' Rebekah's mother says. 'God bless you and Beky. I always keep you in my prayers.'

Delightful, he thinks.

'How long do you think the two of you might stay on the coast?' she says.

'You should probably ask Rebekah that. I think she likes it more than I do.'

'Oh? Don't you like it?'

'I guess I have mixed feelings. There's too much rain and drizzle. It's like living with a runny nose all year.'

The skin around the woman's neck tightens as she smiles. A pearl on a necklace shifts in the hollow of her throat like a tiny egg about to crack. 'It would be so nice to have you closer.'

'It would,' he says. 'Rebekah definitely misses you.' Of course it's a lie. He knows that Rebekah doesn't want to be any closer to her mother. She's never been close to her—or to her father, who died a few years ago. Her parents had been a hard-working couple, and their emotional life, like their Mennonite faith, followed a straight and narrow path: they rarely expressed warmth or anger or any extremes, so that it was never clear what they felt for her, or what she should feel for them. It was only after she'd grown up and moved out that she realized how disorienting it was to be around them. Like following a broken compass.

Muller's father begins recounting his travels to the Orkneys. Muller excuses himself and crosses the floor. The rose-and-dot pattern on the carpet is dizzying. He recalls that Rebekah had been attracted to him because of his emotional honesty. He was transparent about his feelings, and he'd helped her to understand her own—helped to illuminate the deep and vivid meanings of her inner life. He was the psychological prism of their relationship. All of that ended with Lara.

A couple of Rebekah's aunts smile at him. They're plump women, stuffed in dresses like big deli sandwiches in shiny wrapping. He replies in kind and continues on to the bar. He orders water with ice. His old friend Amos comes up. Amos owns a little dog, a Shar Pei, and looks like one too—the sagging skin between the eyes.

They start chatting and Muller sinks a hand into his pocket. He thumbs the edge of the calling card.

The plan is simple. Go to the basement. Phone her number.

It's after hours and she won't be there. A brief message, a quick hello—then he hangs up.

Rebekah appears at his side. 'Hey, Bek,' he says. 'You remember Amos, don't you? My philosopher friend.'

'Great wedding,' Amos says, picking at a tooth. 'Loved the chicken.'

'Amos does chaos theory.'

'Mull, I just. I need you for a second.'

'What is it? Excuse us, Amos.'

He takes her hand and walks her to the lobby. The main lights are on and the music has been turned down to a murmur. A gang of boys are kneeling on the floor with their shirt tails out, trading hockey cards.

'What's wrong, Bek?'

'I had too much. Things are spinning.'

'You had too much what?'

'Wine.'

'Are you serious? Are you *drunk*?'

'I need some air. Everything's spinning.'

Muller leads her to the coat rack. He finds her coat and wraps it around her, and then guides her out through a side door. Before them is the darkened quad—a snowy rectangle bordered by Burwash Hall. The smell of pot skulks in the air.

He leads her down the steps, holding her arm, and along a pathway toward the Gate House. 'How are you feeling now?' he says. 'Is this helping?'

'I'm a bit woozy.'

'What were you thinking, Bek? You can't drink like that. This is our wedding day. You can't get *sloshed*.'

They stop under an arched passage. Her chin is crumpled and tears are running down her face. 'Everything is going to be fine,' he says, brushing her cheek. 'We're together and everything's fine. Please don't cry. Everything's okay.'

'You didn't write a poem,' she whispers.

'What?'

'I thought—I thought you were going to write a poem.'

'You thought I was going to write a poem?'

'For the wedding.'

'Ah. Well. It did cross my mind, Bek. But it's not that easy to write poems. Look, I'll write you something when we get back home, okay? I'll write a good one. I promise.' He cups her face in his hands. 'You look so lovely tonight.'

'Are we going to have a baby?'

'What?'

'I just want to know.'

'I'm sure it'll happen,' he says with a delicate laugh. 'We don't need to discuss this now, do we?'

'Okay.' She gnaws on her lip. 'I just want to know if—'

'You want to know what?'

'If you want one.'

'Bek, listen, it's our wedding day. You've had too much to drink. It's not the time for—'

'You don't want one!' she moans, thumping her fists on his chest.

He grabs her hands. 'Bek, Bek, how could you say that? That is false. That is ridiculous! I do want a family. You know that—haven't I always said that?'

She draws a trembling breath.

'Okay, Bek? Now let's just calm down.'

He lets go of her hands. She presses her face into them. She begins sobbing.

'Bek, listen to me. Tonight is about you and me.'

She shakes her head. He puts his arms around her and she blubbers against his shoulder. He knows it's all his fault, this drunken flood of insecurity. She must have sensed his unfaithfulness. When you lie to people long enough they can smell it on you, that reek of betrayal.

As she presses closer, her shoulders jolting with each sob, he becomes aware of the calling card in his pocket. It's wedged between his thigh and a set of keys for a rented Buick.

He shifts his hip outward, relieving the sensation, and holds Rebekah more tightly in a sideways hug. She quiets to a sniffle.

'You okay, Bek?'

She pulls away from him. There's a splash on the pavement like the squirt of a garden hose.

'Oh God,' she mutters, and pukes out another volley. Fluid and chunks. He clenches his teeth and looks away, swallowing back a gag reflex. A boomerang of moon is caught in the branches of a tree. He looks back at her and she's bent over and panting, her cloudy breath dissolving in the cold air.

The puddle on the ground is steaming. A gob of drool is hanging from her lips. He finds a handkerchief in his pocket.

'Bring me to the bathroom,' she says.

'Are you sure it's all out? You've got a bit hanging there.'

She swipes it away with her hand. 'Just take me.'

He leads her to a bathroom in the basement. Her eyes are pools of smeared make-up. She looks like a circus clown after a bad drug trip.

He hurries to the dining hall and returns with her purse and one of her friends. Rebekah's bridal face is soon repaired, although she still looks pale. They tell everyone she got food poisoning. She remains at the head table for the rest of the evening, sipping water and smiling dully.

They spend the night at a local B&B. She falls asleep instantly while he lies awake beside her, under the four-poster canopy, his head still pounding, playing drum solos of remorse.

He made the phone call. He got her answering machine and said hello and he hates himself for it. He wishes he'd confessed to Rebekah. He should have done it weeks ago, when it would have been so much easier.

Maybe he still can? Maybe it's not too late?

Confess.

Tell the truth.

After all, it wasn't all that scandalous, this thing with Lara. He didn't sleep with her. He never said he loved her. He didn't even kiss her. There was, admittedly, the episode with the prosthetic, not to mention the poem and the phone call, but these minor incidents can be omitted from any confession. What, then, did he really *do* with Lara? What is the substance of his sin?

He hugged her in a storage room. *Hugged* for goodness' sake! His so-called affair was almost nothing, almost laughable, a mere 'peccadillo' as the Catholics might say.

But who is he kidding?

Rebekah would be crushed. Utterly.

Even if their relationship survived, she'd probably never

get over the hurt. Does he want to risk that? A lifetime of lingering resentment?

What he really needs to do is *end* the affair.

Why, why, *why* did he call her? Why can't he face reality? You're married, Muller!

Married: the word is so prickly, like a wool sweater that he'll never be able to take off.

He drifts into a restless sleep. The next morning Rebekah apologizes for getting drunk. The week was so stressful, she tells him. The wedding day overwhelmed her. There's no mention of babies, no mention of the poem. It seems she's forgotten that part of the evening—and that, at least, is a small relief.

They spend their honeymoon in Toronto. They visit friends and cafés and antiquarian bookstores. On a whim they join a protest march against the invasion of Iraq. He's still brooding about Lara, about how he might break things off, although by the final day of the honeymoon he can't fool himself anymore. He wants to see her again. How could he pretend otherwise? He wants to hold her and lose himself in those reckless feelings. He remembers the prosthetic with a shudder of excitement.

But where will they meet?

The question burns in him as he looks out the window of the plane and sees the white rim of tides embracing the cliffs.

The jet wheels around, skidding through cloud, and as it rights itself again, tilting the other way, he spots the hospital building through the flickering light. A red brick tower with a grey extension. Of course they can't see each other anywhere on hospital grounds, or in any public place. They can't risk any more rumours. They'll have to be more cautious from now on.

He recalls, then, certain motels at the edge of town, certain brick-and-vinyl establishments with faded green doorways and shrouded windows. Dens of secrecy, each equipped with a wide, comfy bed.

They'll end up having sex, no doubt, if they meet in a place like that—although the prospect is less threatening now that Muller is married. He feels more secure in his relationship with Rebekah. Is that why he held off on Lara so long? To get married first?

The wisdom of the penis. How shrewd.

The plane touches down with a gentle thump.

He walks down the polished corridor. He rounds the corner and pauses at the door of the physiotherapy gym. The first patients of the morning have arrived. A man in a wheelchair is curling dumb-bells. Lara is at her desk in the back office. Muller's longing convulses in his chest. She turns and sees him and the feeling tightens around his heart like a snake. He wants her so much—all of her, all of her.

She's watching him and her mouth is moving. She's telling him something.

All of me.

Amazing. She's reading his mind.

No—*Call me.*

He nods and hurries back to his office. He's shaking and

flushed and this is the drug, the thing he can't let go of—this wild shiver, this mad hope.

He looks at his hand, his quivering fingers. The wedding ring is a thin band of white gold. Rebekah suggested a thicker one, but he insisted that he liked the thin one.

Thin—a lack of commitment.

He wrenches it off his finger. He tries to place it on the desk, in a bare corner, but the ring sticks to his sweaty hand and falls away.

It bounces off the desktop and jingles onto the floor.

He leaves it there, too hurried to retrieve it, and takes the phone and calls Lara's extension.

She answers immediately.

'Hey there,' he says coolly. 'It's Muller.'

'Hold on a second.' He hears the door close. Her hair rustles warmly against the phone. 'So you're back.'

'Yeah. Flew in yesterday. Did you get my message?'

'I got it.'

'I would have called earlier in the day, but, you know.'

'And how did it go?'

'The big event? Oh, it was okay I guess. How's everything here? Any rumours?'

'No. Haven't noticed anything.' There's a flatness in her voice.

'Are you alright?' he says.

'I went for a walk on your wedding day. A long walk. I had time to think about everything.'

'To think about what?'

'Well—I think it's best if we kept our distance.'

'Kept our distance?'

'Yeah.'

He stares out the window. Fog is rolling over the far hills, and an image is forming in his mind—something poetic. Something anguished. He says, 'To be honest I sort of agree with you, Lara. I was thinking about everything too, you know. And given the circumstances.'

'I just think it's best.'

'Although I did call you. I promised to call and I did.'

'And I don't think we should talk again.'

'What?'

'It has to end here. I'm sorry.'

'Can't we just be—'

'I have to go now. I'm sorry. I've got a patient.'

The line clicks. The dial tone begins droning. He hangs up and looks at the wedding ring on the floor. He picks it up, and closes his hand around it, and notices the distant hills again. The fog is rolling over them, and the image comes to him now.

It's like a blanket, he thinks. Like a blanket on a woman's hip, covering it up.

PART TWO

'So I've decided,' Rebekah says. 'I'm going on a pilgrimage next year.'

It's a warm night in July. She and Muller are having supper at the Ashfields' house. She didn't intend to make the announcement tonight—the pilgrimage is still more an idea than a plan—but it's hard for Rebekah to contain her excitement, especially during these get-togethers. If the four friends were a jazz quartet, then she'd be the unpredictable saxophone, blaring out her thoughts in sudden riffs.

'A pilgrimage?' Evelyn says.

'It's called the Camino—it's in Spain. I read about it in the paper. You walk through the countryside from village to village. You sleep in hostels.'

'Of course she's not meaning to go for *religious* reasons,' Muller says. 'She just likes to walk.'

'Yes, only to walk,' Rebekah laughs. 'I'm not turning Catholic or anything.'

'Are you going alone?' Evelyn says.

'Well, I asked Muller—'

'She knows I have bad knees.'

'But I did ask.'

'Bad patellas. Left and right.'

'You could still try. Imagine the scenery—the Spanish countryside.'

'Patella pain would eclipse the scenery.'

'He doesn't want to sleep at pilgrim's hostels.'

'*Pilgrim's patella pain*. Say that five times fast.'

'It's not a joke, Mull.'

'Do you really want to sleep at a hostel? Think of the bedbugs.'

Evelyn fills her wine glass. 'We were in Seville once. The heat was so oppressive we took shelter in a cathedral.'

'So you preferred the oppression of religion to the oppression of the weather?' Muller says.

'It would seem so,' she smiles. 'Would anyone like the last of this wine?'

'Please,' he says, holding out his glass.

Something nudges Rebekah's toe.

She looks up and meets Sebastian's eye. He's sitting across the table.

She shifts her foot away.

Muller sniffs his glass. 'What's the nose here? I never get the nose.'

'Burnt toast,' Evelyn says. 'And something mousey.'

'Burnt toast and mousey?' He sniffs again, and takes a sip. 'Sorry, I don't detect any rodents having breakfast in here. What about you, Bek?'

She takes her glass and sniffs. 'Yeah. I'm getting it.'

'It seems I have no appreciation for wine. Only words.'

'Maybe we ought to taste a bottle of poetry?' Evelyn says.

'Ah, yes! A wonderful idea! Do you have any T.S. Eliot down in the wine cellar? Some vintage *Waste Land*, perhaps?'

Rebekah feels another prod beneath the table. She looks at Sebastian. Looks away. Her gaze flits across the bookshelf, over paperbacks and volumes of psychoanalysis and across the panelled walls and back to the man's face. He's listening to Evelyn and his toe is nestled against the side of Rebekah's heel. It doesn't make sense. Does he think she's the table leg?

'By the way, how is your writing going?' Evelyn asks Muller. 'Didn't you say that you'd started working on a novel?'

'It's half novel and half memoir. I'm blurring the boundaries. You know, I came upon a curious memoir recently...'

She glances at Sebastian. Muller is rambling about a British diplomat. He can't remember the name. Sebastian's toe is still there, a bulge of flesh, pressed against her. He isn't wearing socks and she can feel the hardness of his toenail against her skin. Muller is stuck on the name—it's like the name of a city—and he looks at Rebekah and asks if she can remember. 'No,' she mumbles, and she's about to sip her wine when Sebastian's toe gives her another baffling nudge.

'It was during the war,' Muller says.

'Which war?' Evelyn says.

'Halifax—that's it. Lord Halifax. During the Second World War. So this Lord Halifax, the story goes, is arriving at a diplomatic meeting, and he looks out the window of his car and sees this man. It's Adolf Hitler, but Halifax notices the uniform and thinks, *Oh, this must be the footman.'*

'Is this a true story?'

'Yes. He mistook Hitler for a servant. But I can imagine that. You see a short man in uniform with a trim little moustache.'

'The kind of man you can trust with your coat,' Sebastian says.

'Exactly. *Good day, Führer. Would you hang this in the closet, please?'*

Laughter.

She drinks and glances at him. God, why did she glance? His toe starts brushing the side of her foot. Is it because she glanced? Did she give him permission? His toe is brushing, stroking, licking her like a dry tongue, and she doesn't want it. She shouldn't want it.

Goose bumps blossom across her leg. The warmth spreads through her thighs and swells into her face, and she gazes down at her plate.

A crust of bread. Picked bones.

He strokes her through dessert. She takes away her foot from time to time, but then she puts it back and he finds her. He won't leave her alone. She's afraid and naked and flattered. She walks home later in a daze, her face turned up at the drizzle that's falling through the street lights, pecking at her cheeks, her lips.

She lies awake in bed, listening to rain on the rooftop.

He's attracted to her, yes. She always suspected it, even

hoped for it, although this is something unexpected. He's never made such overtures before. He's always been proper, one could say formal. Is he actually interested in her? Does he do this with other women? Isn't he happy with Evelyn?

The rain on the roof—she listens. The sound is like a thousand small hands knocking on a door.

Is *she* attracted to *him*? Here's the real question, the one that's crouching behind all the others. She knows the answer, of course—has always known the answer—although her feelings for Sebastian are usually obscured behind her admiration for the Ashfields as a couple. Even now, she can almost pretend that what she feels for him is only that—a minor aspect of something larger and more innocent.

Muller stirs under the blankets. She stares at him while the sound of the rain, the insistent pattering, fills her ears.

She has no intention of telling him. If she can't understand it herself, then how could she explain it? And to speak of it would spoil it, this feeling of what happened. Like a heart full of doves, waiting to be set free.

Sebastian plays footsies every time they visit for supper. At first she tells herself not to respond, but soon she's replying with her own little strokes. She doesn't think of it as flirting. It's another form of conversation. It sweetens the friendship. It goes on all summer, and she begins to notice a space opening up inside of her, a vast and warm space like an undiscovered room in a mansion, that is meant only for him and her and these beautiful moments.

She starts taking the Number 3 bus to the university

where she works as an administrator, knowing that he rides the same bus to the General. She catches it at the corner down the road from the apartment, and from there the bus lumbers into the downtown and stops in front of The Tin Cup, where he waits.

She takes her leather bag off the seat beside her. He climbs on board and they exchange kisses on the cheek—their usual custom. He sits down and they start chatting. He never brings up what happens under the table, never even hints at it, but she isn't surprised. Sebastian Ashfield isn't the sort of person who talks about the obvious.

The bus ride is fifteen minutes and she blathers through most of it, often about the novels she's reading, mostly authors he's recommended. South American writers, African writers, Indian writers—writers from hot climates. Or else she talks about the pilgrimage.

'I've decided I'm going in April,' she says one morning. 'Late April or early May.'

'So you're really going to do it? That's very exciting, Rebekah.'

'I'll have to cover about twenty kilometres a day.'

'You'll have to pack light, I guess. No wine bottles?'

'No, and no hair products either. Some people rip the pages out of books after reading them, just to make them lighter.'

'What sacrilege.'

The bus halts, the bag slides off her knees. They reach for it together and their hands brush.

'I forgot to mention,' she says. 'I found some great books

at the library with pictures of the trail. I left them at work but I'll bring them next time.'

'I'd love to see them, Rebekah. Listen, why don't you bring them to my office some day? Maybe over the lunch hour? You're only across the road.'

She looks out at the harbour hills. She sees the rusted fuel tanks, like bleeding stumps on the rocky slope. 'Okay,' she says.

'What day works for you?'

'Well, any day I guess.'

'Then how about today?'

'Today.'

'Yes. Unless you're busy?'

The invitation takes her off guard. It's hard to say no—not that she wants to say no. She wants to be his friend. Just a friend. She's not looking for anything else.

He tells her it's complicated to get to his office and suggests they meet at the hospital gift shop. She arrives early, before noon, and looks at a shelf full of teddy bears. She tries not to think about Muller, tries not to think about how she'll explain herself if somebody she knows catches her here—although, really, there's nothing wrong with this. She's only meeting with a friend. She could even say she was going to an appointment with her doctor, or leaving an appointment. Her mind is full of possibilities, cushioned, distracted. The teddy bears watch her silently.

Sebastian's face looms out of a silver balloon.

'Waiting long?' he says as she turns suddenly.

'Oh hi. Just got here.'

'Great. It's right this way.'

She follows him down the corridor. He walks slightly ahead, like a doctor leading a patient. They enter a new section of the building and go down a spiral staircase, circling a steel double helix that's suspended from wires and gleaming in the light of a glass dome above.

'I never saw that before,' she says. 'That's neat.'

Oh God—not *neat*.

Impressive. Striking.

She follows him through a pair of green doors. Beyond is a bare white-walled corridor. At the far end is a sign: Parking Exit. They pass a bathroom and reach another door. There's no name or number on it.

He takes out his keys.

'This is your office?' she says.

'It used to be upstairs but some of my clients complained it was too public. Nobody wants to be seen visiting a psychologist. The stigma, you know.' He opens the door and gestures to a couch. 'Make yourself comfortable.'

The office is a small, lamplit room. She slides the bag off her shoulder and sits stiffly. Sebastian closes the door and settles into a plush swivel chair, hands cupped in his lap. Behind him is a computer, some books, photos of the children on a pebble beach. There are no pictures of Evelyn.

'I had a poster of that once,' Rebekah says, noticing a small print by a bookshelf.

'It's lovely, isn't it? Chagall's work is so magical.'

'Chagall. I didn't realize.' She gives a nervous laugh and

starts unbuckling her bag. 'Anyway, here are all the books.'

'Yes, let's see.'

'This one—this is a travelogue. It's got some nice photos.'

He thumbs through it slowly. She talks and piles the books beside her, worried that she's blathering again.

'There's a detailed map in this one. You can see the whole route and, uh, the topography.'

Topography. *Good* word.

He moves to the couch. She opens the book between them. 'I'll be starting in León, right here.'

'Why León?'

'I've only got three weeks of vacation. It takes about that long to get to Santiago from León. Santiago is where it ends. And here—' She turns a page. 'This is the cathedral. The bones of Saint James are supposed to be buried under it. When I told my mother she said, *Oh, Rebekah, it's probably just a dog's bones.*'

'I would have expected a more positive reaction from your mother. Isn't she religious?'

'She's Mennonite. They don't believe in relics.'

'What do they believe in?'

'Work and prayer, mostly.'

'I suppose they've got it half right.'

There's a hollow clunk in the corridor. Rebekah tenses and looks at the door. 'It's the parking exit,' he says.

'Oh.'

He's gazing at her. She feels helpless, pinned against herself. He takes her hand and she slips it away. 'I'm just a bit. I'm—'

She's half turned, sees the Chagall. A man and woman floating in the blue. He takes her hand and tugs her closer and it's like falling, like tumbling into a pool—a splash of shock and then soundlessness.

The kiss is hardly anything. A light touch. Mostly breath.

'Rebekah,' he whispers.

He shifts closer and pushes the book off the couch and his mouth is warm, tastes of mint. What am I doing. What am I doing. She turns away and notices the book on the floor, the covers spread wide. A golden Spanish field. His breath is on her face. 'I didn't think this would happen,' she whispers.

'Neither did I.'

Her lips come apart and she inhales him. Their tongues meet and she understands the games under the table now. They were a preparation for this—this deeper meeting. He cups her face in his hands. 'I need to know that you can protect this, Rebekah.'

She nods, floundering in his gaze.

'Are you sure? I need to hear it.'

'I'm sure.'

'We need to feel safe. Are you and Muller okay? It's important that you and Muller are okay.'

'We're okay. Are you and Evelyn—?'

'Of course,' he says curtly, as if mildly offended. Then his face softens. 'Now come here.'

She thought they were only going to talk. She didn't think she would end up like this—unbuttoning her blouse.

Her heart, it seems, has no radar.

An hour later she leaves the hospital. She feels his wetness between her legs as she crosses the road to the university. She wipes herself in a bathroom stall in the Modern Languages building and then proceeds to her office, closes the door, looks at the computer. The screen saver is spinning webs of light. The air smells of asphalt. Workers are tarring a roof somewhere.

She spends the rest of the afternoon at her desk, alone, in quiet panic. This is new territory, this thing with Sebastian, although she instantly understands the risks. There will be lies, and she'll tell them. She'll carry them to the grave. She never knew she had an instinct for something like this—this thing, whatever it is. Not an affair.

She won't call it that.

At four thirty she takes the Number 3 home. The odour of Sebastian lingers on her face. The mint gum, the roguish spice of cologne. She opens the front door of the apartment and looks up the stairs and sees Muller's jacket on the coat rack, dangling by the neck.

Yeats meets her on the landing, purring warmly. She gives him a pat and goes into the bathroom and locks the door.

She pushes down her pants and wipes herself again. She rinses her face and gargles with mouthwash. There's a knock at the door as she's smearing on deodorant.

The knob rattles. 'Bek?'

'Yes, hold on.' She glances in the mirror, straightening out her blouse, and then comes out. 'What is it?' she smiles.

'Why did you lock?'

'What kind of question is that? I got home and went to the bathroom.' She flicks off the light and kisses him. 'How was your day? Were you writing?'

'I didn't hear you flush.'

'I didn't flush, Mull, because I was having some feminine trouble. I was actually sick all day. I dropped by the health clinic if you really want to know.'

She walks past him, feigning annoyance, and heads into the kitchen.

'Sorry,' he says, following. 'I didn't realize. Are you okay?'

'I'm fine. But I think I've got cysts.'

'*Cysts?*'

'Ovarian cysts. It's nothing serious.'

'Are you sure? I mean, it sounds serious.'

'Apparently it's common. My mother had them.'

'Did they examine you, or—?'

'The doctor just sort of. Felt around.' She grabs a dirty dish off the table. 'You need to clean up after you eat.'

'So you're okay?'

'He said I'm fine. I feel fine now, just a bit bloated. It's my night for supper, isn't it?'

She goes to the fridge and Muller starts talking about his writing. It's been a good day for him. He's made some breakthroughs in the plot of his novel. She nods and goes to the counter, and squats down and opens a cupboard. Memories of the afternoon erupt behind her eyes and spill down her throat and into her stomach.

She pauses, overwhelmed by the sensuous inner flood,

gazing into the clutter of cookware. 'Anyhow,' Muller says. 'I'm going to head back up for a few minutes. Give me a shout when supper's ready.'

'Sure,' she says.

She listens to his footsteps receding through the hallway and up the stairs—and realizes, with a burst of relief, that she's passed the first test.

The first of many.

She takes out a large pot and goes to the sink. Routine, at least, has a calming effect. Filling the pot with water. Turning on the stove. Chopping garlic into bits.

She needs to remember this. You can hide behind the ordinary. You can disguise yourself in the familiar.

She makes a habit of leaving her office early for the visits. She drinks a bottle of pineapple juice on the way to sweeten her breath. Once in the hospital she heads upstairs to a spacious bathroom on the second floor to check her face and hair, and then descends to Sebastian's corridor. If his door is ajar then she knocks and enters, but if the door is closed— meaning he's with a client—then she slips into the bathroom down the hall. There, she counts to seven, or fifteen, or whatever number pops into her head, and checks the door again. She might go through the routine several times before the door is open.

They take off their shoes and socks first. They settle onto the couch. She leans back on his chest, hooking her arms around his thighs, and he belts his hands under her breasts. It's like they're riding each other down a roller coaster.

Impending thrill. She does most of the talking, as usual, and never knows whether they're going to make love or not. It's all up to him. An unspoken rule. Sometimes they spend the whole hour talking, and sometimes they kiss. Other times he whispers, 'Let's take our clothes off.' There's never any seduction on these occasions. They get up and he clicks off the lamp. Static flickers around their bodies as they undress in the darkness. The lovemaking lasts just a few minutes and always ends when he's finished, and only then does she feel closest to him—when he lies with his head on her belly, eyes closed, his breath brushing over her thigh. His upper body is shaved, down to the crotch. Smooth as a baby.

'Is it okay for you?' she whispers one day.

'Is what okay?'

'When we're together. The way we do it.'

'It's good, Rebekah. Yes. It's wonderful.'

Keys jingle in the corridor. The custodian is opening a storage closet. 'I meant to tell you something,' she says. 'I don't know if it matters. It doesn't matter to me. Not anymore.'

'What is it?'

'When I was a girl. There was this guy, a neighbour.' She squints, holding back tears.

'You were abused?'

'I'm sorry, this is so stupid.'

He slides up to her face. 'You don't have to be sorry, Rebekah. It must have been awful.'

'I only wanted you to know. Sometimes I think it makes me more passive. When I'm making love.'

'Your lovemaking is beautiful. How old were you when it happened?'

'Five.'

'You were so small.' He kisses her softly on the cheek. 'Do you want to tell me about it? Sometimes it helps to talk. If you're comfortable.'

She stares at the slim glow of light under the door. 'He lived down the road,' she says. 'We knew him from church. On some days his wife was supposed to babysit me after school, but she'd leave me with him. She had a night job and slept through the afternoon. That was how it started.'

'What did he do to you?'

'He played doctor. It was like a game—I didn't know the difference. He pretended to fix my arm or put on a bandage. In the end he was putting his finger inside me. It was never violent or anything. Sometimes he masturbated himself. I didn't know what I was looking at. I thought he was peeing himself.'

'How long did all this go on?'

'A few years. Then one day I said no, and that was it. He just stopped.'

'You stood up for yourself.'

'I should have done it sooner. I don't know why I didn't. He'd do those things to me and then an hour later I'd be at the kitchen table saying grace with my parents. It was as if—' She hesitates. She was going to say, As if I lived out of two boxes. Two boxes that were separated, walled off from each other.

'As if what?' he says.

'I knew it was wrong, but a part of me was okay with what he was doing. Not really okay, but—'

'You knew it was wrong, but it felt good?'

'Something like that. I know it sounds weird.'

'Not at all. You were a child, Rebekah. Children don't regard sexual experiences as shameful. Not until they're taught to think so. Shame and guilt are concepts, things we learn from others. Am I the first person you've told?'

'Muller knows. It's never been an issue.'

'But you feel that you're more passive?'

'I know I am. To me, lovemaking is something that gets done to me. Performed on me. Like an operation.'

'Do you dislike it?'

'No—I do like it.' She gives a laugh. 'Especially with you. I just feel like I can't assert myself. Like I don't even want to.'

'If you don't want to, then is it really a problem?'

'That depends. I want to make sure you're happy.'

The door of the storage room thuds. The custodian's keys jingle down the corridor, a sound like chains.

'I am happy, Rebekah. Of course I am.'

The relationship with Sebastian transforms her. She starts spending more time on her clothes and make-up in the morning. She cuts down on sweets, goes to aerobics after work, and prefers the company of her novels over Muller in the evening. On weekends she goes hiking along the cliffs and comes home with her cheeks reddened with windburn, raving about the beauty of it all. Her zest for life is turbocharged. Muller says that she's changed, and she insists that she hasn't—except, maybe, that she's maturing. Enjoying life. Becoming her own person.

'I noticed your Camino books,' he says one day over supper. 'In your bag.'

'What about them.'

'Let me ask you this, Bek. It's only a question. What if some guy tries to hit on you?'

'It's a pilgrimage, Mull, not a pickup joint.'

'But not everyone is going to be a saint.'

'I'm going there to *walk*.'

'You're going to be on a dirt road in northern Spain for what, four weeks?'

'Three weeks.'

'Whatever. It's a long time. There are going to be men around. Don't you think these guys might—?'

'Mull.'

'They'll talk to you. They'll try to make moves on you.'

'I can handle myself.'

'But these guys—you need to understand, Bek—they'll be lonely spiritual types. You know the type? Desperate to fill the inner void. If they can't do it with God, they'll do it with a woman. It would be different if you were going with somebody.'

'I invited you but you weren't interested.'

'It's not that I'm not interested. My knees—I told you. Anyhow, I'm just concerned. You're my wife.'

Wife: the word burns in her ears. 'I find this whole conversation offensive, you know.'

'I want you to be careful. That's all I'm asking.'

'I'll be careful, alright? Now can we drop this subject?'

She flies to Spain at the end of April. She walks for four hours each day carrying a fifteen-pound backpack. The pilgrimage trail is a path of dirt and stone. Sometimes it runs parallel with country roads and highways, but often it departs and goes its own way, cutting through farm fields or circling around a misty hill or dipping into the grassy folds of the horizon—a reddish line of earth that stretches forever before her. It's the only constant, this line. The residue of a thousand years of devout footsteps. She sees mountains smothered in wildflowers and wanders through eucalyptus forests that smell of cough candy. She hears the chanting of monks drifting out of stone churches and sees storks gliding onto thatched rooftops—and always the dirt line stretches before her. The entire country sways to the rhythm of her stride. Spain is her pendulum, and the steady crunch of her hiking shoes lulls her into something like prayer.

The feet are holy.

Here's a doctrine she can believe in.

It's early in the pilgrimage season and there are few people on the trail. She meets a group of Spaniards, all young men, and often joins them for supper at the hostels. They flatter her and make overtures, which she always deflects, and she gives herself credit for it: she's watching out for herself, just as she promised Muller.

She walks alone, starting out early each morning. The route takes her through Hospital de Órbigo, Astorga, Rabanal, the ruins of Foncebadón, and up a snow-blotched, windy mountain to a place called Cruz de Ferro. It's not a village, just a heap of rocks with a post rising out of it, topped with a cross. A place where people leave stones that represent their burdens and sins. Water bottles and shoes and other junk have also been tossed onto the pile.

The wind is freezing. She gazes up at the cross. With a flick of her hand she tosses a stone. It clinks and clatters among the rocks.

She walks on.

A day later she phones Sebastian from one of the villages. The line is crackling and she can barely hear him.

'We're leaving tomorrow,' he says. 'Are you on schedule?'

'I am. I'll try to be there.'

'You'll *try*?'

'I can't predict everything. I still have a week on the trail.'

'Rebekah, I'm sensing a doubt.'

'I'm only saying—'

'If it's too complicated then I need to know.'

'It's not too complicated. That's not what I meant. I'll be there.'

They're going to meet in Paris. The Ashfields, as it happens, will be in the city visiting Evelyn's sister during the same week that Rebekah is finishing the pilgrimage in Spain. The opportunity is too delicious to resist—a rendezvous in the city of romance. But the timing will be tight. She has to take a bus and make it to Paris before they fly on to England.

She reaches Santiago on the nineteenth of May, as planned. She gets her pilgrim's certificate at the cathedral and slips into the church service. An organ is playing with a heavenly gloom and monks in dark robes are gathered in a circle, pulling down on a long rope that holds the *botafumeiro*. It's a giant smoking censer. The bronze, bell-shaped vessel hangs from the ceiling and swings back and forth over the crowd, higher and higher with each pull of the rope, wafting grey clouds of incense—an ancient tradition meant to quell the awful stench of the pilgrims.

It reminds Rebekah of how grubby she is. She needs to pretty herself up for Paris.

She squeezes her way toward the exit. She wanders through the shopping district for a few hours in search of a nice outfit. That night she goes to a bar with the Spaniards.

'Will you come to Finisterre tomorrow?' asks one of them. 'There we burn our clothes and celebrate.'

'No,' says another. 'She goes to Paris.'

'Paris?' says the first. 'But why you go to Paris, Angelita?'

Angelita is their nickname for her: Little Angel.

'I've always wanted to see Paris,' she says.

'Maybe she has a boyfriend,' calls out another, a young man named Emilio. The others begin whooping and banging the table.

'I do *not* have a boyfriend,' she says. 'I'm married, re-member?'

'But you must stay one more day.'

'I should be getting to bed. I'm tired.'

'No, no!' they cry. 'Angelita!'

She pulls some money from her pocket to pay for her drinks. A grey stone falls out and clatters onto the floor.

Sebastian had given it to her before she left—something to remember him by while they were apart.

'Hey!' Emilio says. 'Don't you go to Cruz de Ferro? You have to throw your stone away. You have to throw away your sins. That is the rule. Look everybody, she don't throw away her stone!'

'Sinner, sinner!' they laugh.

Rebekah takes the stone. 'I threw away another stone,' she says with a wink. 'I kept this one for the sins I like.'

'Oh, she's a good one!' they cry. 'She's a good one!'

She puts some euros on the table.

'No, no, no,' Emilio says. 'We pay. But stay with us.'

'I need to go to bed. I'm very tired.'

'But this night is so special!'

She leaves the bar and heads down the road. A minute later she hears someone running behind her. She looks back and sees Alfonso—one of the Spaniards. The quiet one of the group. He has her father's eyes, gentle and brown, a pair of almonds.

'You cannot walk alone,' he says. 'It's no safe.'

'But the *refugio* is very close.'

'No, I come.'

They cross an empty courtyard. 'Angelita, may I speak you something?'

'*Tell* you something.'

'*Sí.* Tell you something.'

'What is it?'

He stops. 'We sit, okay?'

'Okay.'

They sit on a bench. A lilac tree hangs over them, tangled against the black sky, dripping sweetness into the air.

'What is it, Alfonso?'

'Why you go tomorrow?'

'Well, that was my plan.'

'But you must come to Finisterre.'

'Is that what you wanted to tell me?'

'No. I want to tell.' He shakes his head. 'I want to say. *Say?*'

'Yes.'

'I want to say your husband is lucky. You are beautiful and he is lucky.'

'Thank you, Alfonso. Is that all?'

'*Sí.*'

She's about to get up when he touches her hand.

'What?' she says.

'Can I kiss you, Angelita?'

'No,' she laughs.

'Why you laugh?'

'I'm sorry, you guys are so forward.'

'I marry you. Please.'

'That's sweet, Alfonso. Thank you. Now I need to go to bed.'

He follows her through the darkness and up a stone stairway. She's flattered by his interest, of course, and by all the overtures she's gotten over the past few weeks, but it means nothing. It's merely pleasant—pleasant and crude, like their Spanish table wine.

They reach the *refugio* and follow a corridor to her

room. It's the first private room she's had during the journey.

'I come in?' he says, as she unlocks the door.

'No, you may not.'

'Your husband is lucky man. So lucky. When I see you, my heart.' He grabs his shirt at the chest, muttering to himself.

'You're very sweet, Alfonso.'

'One kiss. Please.'

She leans over and pecks him on the cheek. 'Okay?'

'So fast, Angelita!'

'What were you expecting?'

'I—' He looks at his feet. He looks up. 'I wish I marry you.'

'Unfortunately it's too late.'

'I marry you and I give you everything. Everything! It's no lie. My father has big factory. One day it's my factory.'

'What kind of factory?'

'Cat food factory.'

She laughs.

'Why you laugh?'

'I'm not laughing at you. I just never knew anybody who made cat food.'

'It's big company. You be with me and I give you everything, everything.' He's clutching at his heart.

'There are lots of other girls for you, Alfonso.'

'They are not like you,' he says, moving closer.

She puts a hand on his chest. 'I'll see you tomorrow, alright?'

'*Sí*,' he sighs. 'We rent car and go to Finisterre? Please?'

'Alright. Maybe.'

'We see the ocean. We rent car together, just you and me. Best car—I have money. Okay, Angelita?'

'Yes, maybe we can do that.'

'Will you kiss me? Please? I ask for this one thing. I ask only for something small, so small.'

She pecks him on the edge of the mouth. He slips his arms around her waist and tries for another. She turns her face away and he pushes her into the room. It's like a clumsy, backwards waltz.

They bump against the open door. His tongue slips into her mouth. She turns away.

'Please,' he whispers.

'No.'

'A kiss—a small kiss.'

He kisses her and she struggles to push him back and he starts thrusting against her, murmuring desperately. He smells of bar smoke and old sweat and she notices a window across the room. It's arched like two hands in prayer.

Sebastian flashes through her mind.

Sebastian—watching her with a thin smile.

He has too much control over her. She can admit it now. She's weak. Flimsy. She needs him too much and resents him for that. Why the hell can't she be stronger? Alfonso gives a moan. His body relaxes and she punches at his chest and shoves him into the corridor.

He's holding his crotch, half squatting like a boy who needs to pee. 'Oh Angelita,' he says dreamily.

She slams the door. Bolts it.

She walks to the bed, then turns and walks back to the door.

'You ass!' she cries.

It was an unfortunate incident, but she doesn't let herself dwell on it. The next morning she checks out early and wanders the city until her eleven-thirty bus departs. She sits in the back, gazing out the window. Fields and villages flash by. Machine gun fire blasts out of a TV set over the aisle. It takes four hours to reach León where she started the pilgrimage three weeks ago, and by evening the bus is climbing the Pyrenees.

The air conditioning is on and she can't sleep from the cold. Her calves are swollen from sitting so long. She finds a section of an English newspaper tucked beside the seat and browses through a story about a psychotherapist who slept with his clients. *Psychotherapist*, she reads tiredly. *Psychotherapist. Psychotherapist. Psycho the rapist.*

The bus stops at the border to change drivers. A pastel pink light is seeping into the sky. She stares at the passing fields and towns and tree-lined avenues and walls of graffiti. A suburb of apartment blocks signals the outskirts of the city. The bus creeps through traffic for over an hour before pulling into the station.

She's here at last. Paris! Whatever doubts she had about coming here, whatever resentment about Sebastian—it's all swept away in the excitement. She finds a bathroom and changes into a fresh T-shirt, and then turns her underwear inside out (a trick she learned on the pilgrimage when there was no time to launder). She catches a city bus and takes it a few stops before deciding to walk the rest of the way, hoping to work the swelling out of her legs.

The buildings with their faded ornamentation remind her of old wedding cakes that are slowly melting. One of the big avenues leads her to the Rue de Rivoli where she finds her hotel. It's a modest establishment, the thin wedge of a larger building.

The woman at the reception desk peers over a newspaper.

'Good day, Madam,' Rebekah says in her best French. 'I have a reservation for tonight. Tonight and tomorrow night. Rebekah Raymer.'

The woman's nose is a white door knocker of bone. Her nostrils tighten as she studies Rebekah's passport. She slides over a key and Rebekah takes the stairs to the fourth floor, leaping them two at a time.

Her room is a luxury compared to the dorm-style lodgings in Spain. She's got her own bathroom, a large bed, and a balcony facing the cluttered rooftops of the city.

She takes her first hot shower in weeks and then slips into her new clothes—a knee-length linen skirt, a sleeveless white shirt, and a cotton blouse with mother-of-pearl buttons.

Feeling refreshed and beautiful again, she heads out of the hotel with a camera pouch as a purse. It's early afternoon and the sky is overcast, the colour of stone dust. Guided by her city map, she makes her way to the Notre Dame Cathedral—the place they'll rendezvous—working out the route she'll follow tomorrow morning. Tourists are milling about the plaza and looking up at the stone figures on the walls—an assembled nightmare of kings, saints, and gargoyles. She has lunch at a café on the other side of the Seine and then wanders along the river.

She ventures into a department store on the Champs-Élysées and buys lipstick, a razor, and a pair of stringy underwear, burgundy-coloured to match the hotel curtains. Outside again, she goes to a sidewalk café and orders coffee and a slice of Alsatian pie.

Sipping on her cup, she observes the congested avenue. How distracted everybody looks. On the pilgrimage she could walk for hours without seeing anyone. She became accustomed to solitude for the first time in her life, was storing it up inside of her—vast silences, huge tracts of Galician landscape—and now she's losing it.

She imagines telling all this to Sebastian, tangled up in the hotel bed. The waiter brings her the bill.

'Sixteen euros?' she says.

'*Oui,*' he replies smartly.

She thinks of her bank account. She'll have to throw out next month's statement in case Muller snoops through her mail.

She leaves the café and strolls through the Tuileries Gardens and finds her way back to Rue de Rivoli. She goes into another store and buys a new pair of sandals, fairly priced. She crosses the river along the Boulevard du Palais and comes to a long queue of tourists going into a court-yard. It's the Sainte-Chapelle. Sebastian once told her that the stained glass was gorgeous. She wonders if she ought to go inside and take a look, just to be able to say, Yes, it was gorgeous. Then she sees him coming down the sidewalk. He's looking at her with a glint of surprise. Kate is in his arms and Evelyn is next to him, wearing sunglasses, holding David's hand. The boy is dressed in the same white shirt and tan casuals as his father. Such a dashing family.

Evelyn's face is angled toward the boulevard and Rebekah glances about for an escape. The traffic is heavy and she can't cross the road. She turns her face down and sees dog poo on the sidewalk. A brown coil smudged by a heel.

I finished the pilgrimage early, she'll tell them. Figured I'd see Paris.

That's her excuse—her lie. These constant lies.

They pass to her left, a blur of terror. 'Aunt Beky!' calls one of the children, but the words are faint and maybe imagined. Lost in the din of a passing motorcycle.

After a minute she looks back and they're gone.

She hurries back to the hotel, anxious and wishing she'd never gone out. What if they *did* see her—Evelyn or the children? He may not show up tomorrow. This whole effort might be a waste. She should never have agreed to come to Paris. What was she thinking? All the money and pressure and lies—and for what? A few hours of sex and croissants?

She has no appetite that evening and goes to bed early, fretting, exhausted. She dreams of Cruz de Ferro. She's sitting at the foot of the cross, putting stones in her mouth, swallowing them one by one.

The room is gleaming when she wakens. She squints at the clock and realizes it's late. She throws off the blanket, takes a quick shower, gets dressed. She hurries down the stairs in her new sandals.

It's after ten o'clock when she reaches the Notre Dame. She scans the plaza and can't see him. She hurries into the cathedral. The place feels familiar, like the churches of the pilgrimage. A warehouse of stillness. Tourists are staring mutely upward and a woman in a shawl is hunched in a chair, forehead pressed on her knuckles. Rebekah walks up the middle aisle. She gazes up at one of the rose windows. The petals are dizzying and her foot is stinging. Her heel is raw, chafed by the new sandals.

Three hundred kilometres with hardly a blister, she'll tell him. And now this.

She goes outside and heads to a bench. She brushes away some flower blossoms. He must have been held up by the children. He must have missed the metro.

An old man with a cane grins at her. There's salad in his teeth like moss in a wall. She reapplies her lipstick. She fusses with her hair and checks her watch. She looks back and forth across the plaza.

The realization that he isn't coming descends on her reluctantly, with pricks of pain, like needles pressing into her heart. Her heart is a pincushion.

He doesn't love her. He's never loved her.

But she always knew that, didn't she?

Pigeons are waddling around her bench, cooing sadly. She glances up at the cathedral, that glorious and indifferent mass of stone, a nest of gargoyles, and notices one of them high up, leaping frozenly into the sky.

What an ass.

She kicks away the birds and starts back to the hotel.

She catches the next plane home via New York. There's no email from him, no explanation, but it doesn't matter. She's through with him. *Finished*.

Eight days later he returns from Europe and invites her to his office. She's there at noon in her Paris outfit, faintly resentful, her breath sweetened with pineapple juice.

After sex they lounge on the couch. She talks about the pilgrimage but makes no mention of Paris, waiting for him to bring it up.

And how can he *not* say anything? How can he just ignore it?

'There was this Spanish guy,' she says. 'He kept coming on to me. I had to tell him off.'

'Hmm,' he says sleepily.

The air vent drones. A cool draft is falling on her shoulders. 'I waited for you in Paris,' she says. 'I waited a long time.'

'I did my best, Rebekah.'

'I went through a lot to be there.'

'Don't you think I tried?'

'I had to lie to Muller, I had to hide things—'

'Don't you think I *tried*?'

'I'm not saying that you didn't try. But it wasn't easy for me either.'

He peels himself off her body abruptly, like a bandage. He takes his pants from the chair. She sits up and tears are running down her cheeks. She finds her bra on the floor and brushes off a clump of dust. 'It's hard living like this,' she sniffles. 'I'm doing my best but it's hard.'

He buttons up his shirt, stern-faced, and waits by the door as she gets her clothes on. She slings her bag onto her shoulder. 'I'm sorry,' she whispers.

'Yes. Well. I'm going to have to think about things, Rebekah. I think we both need some time to think about things.'

The words slam into her like a wrecking ball. He stops calling her. He stops taking the Number 3 to work. Evelyn suffers from a succession of migraines around the same time, suspending the usual supper visits. Sebastian plays squash at the university on Thursdays and Rebekah resorts to spying on him from a glassed-in corridor above the courts. The sight of him is enough to fill her with a familiar ache, a familiar comfort, and almost makes her believe that she could carry on if she had only this—an occasional glimpse.

She's reading a book one afternoon, sipping Sebastian's favourite whiskey, when Muller comes into the living room. 'What book is that?' he says.

'*The Library of Babel*.'

'By Borges?'

'Yes.'

He walks to the window. 'You seem down lately, Bek. What's going on?'

'I'm tired.'

'Are you upset because they haven't invited us in a while?'

She flips a page.

'I think we depend on them too much,' he says. 'Sebastian and Evelyn. Don't you think?'

She glances over the top of the book. Muller is gazing across the road. The sky is a flimsy roof of cloud with orange drips of light seeping through the cracks. 'We look up to them too much,' he goes on. 'Not that I mean to be critical. I suppose there are good reasons to look up to them. They're intelligent and sophisticated, and then those accents—gives everything they say a ring of nobility. You feel inferior in their presence, yet privileged.'

'What are you talking about.'

'I'm saying there are reasons why we look up to them, Bek. But I doubt the feeling is mutual.'

'You don't know that.'

'Look at how we mimic them. The wine and the cigars and the malt whiskey. The quaint expressions like *I shall*. When did we ever talk like that? *I shall*.'

'I don't like you analyzing our friends.'

'I'm not analyzing our friends, I'm analyzing *us*. Look at the book you're reading. You wouldn't care about world literature if it wasn't for them—or *him*, I should say. I used to recommend books and you were never interested.'

'I read whatever you gave me.'

'But you weren't interested. Then he recommends Borges and you're all over it. Since when would you have ever read Borges? I mean, do you even *understand* Borges?'

'I don't have to listen to this.'

'You've obviously got a blind spot on this issue.'

'I said I'm *not* going to listen.'

'Oh yes you are! Because I am your *husband*,' he says with sudden righteousness. 'Because this is a marriage. Because—'

She gets up and heads out of the room.

'You walk away and it's over!'

She continues down the hallway.

'That's it! We're finished! No—wait. Bek, I'm sorry!'

She snatches her handbag off the floor by the shoe mat and notices the grey stone inside—the stone that Sebastian gave her. It's nestled amid a wad of crumpled tissues. She was weeping yesterday.

Muller comes hurrying into the hallway. 'I didn't mean that. I'm sorry.'

She snaps the bag shut. 'How could you talk like that?'

'I was jealous—I'm sorry. I don't know what's wrong with me. I've been feeling insecure lately. Please, Bek.'

'Don't ever say things like that again. Ever.'

There's no further discussion. She stomps back to the living room and takes up her book, her whiskey. Muller keeps his distance for the rest of the day and offers to make supper that evening, evidently trying to make up for his outburst.

It came as a total surprise to Rebekah. She didn't realize he was jealous, or even suspicious. She almost wishes that he accused her of something. It would have been easier to let go of Sebastian. To decide that the relationship *is* over, by *her* choice. That it really *is* time to move on.

Isn't it?

Or has she completely forgotten her resentment?

Two days later the Englishman invites her back to his office. He doesn't apologize for cutting her off. He doesn't even mention it, and she dares not bring it up, not wanting to upset him. Not wanting to risk another punishment. She's like a prisoner who was freed for a while but is somehow relieved to be back in the cell.

From now on his invitations come only once every couple of weeks—less than in the past. The other days, the in-between days, she waits, quietly boiling with longing and worry.

The summer arrives reluctantly, drizzling through June, but July manages to shake it off and the sun finally bursts through, smothering the coast with precious warmth.

Rebekah and Muller rent a cabin by the sea with the Ashfields one weekend. It's only the second or third time they've all gotten together since the Ashfields returned from Europe—Evelyn's migraines have continued to flare up more than usual.

The couples are at the beach one afternoon, and Evelyn is talking about her sister's ex-husband, when Rebekah feels something brush against the back of her thigh.

A blade of grass, it seems.

It can only be Sebastian. He's lying behind her. No one but the gulls drifting overhead can see what's going on, which prompts Rebekah to reflect, with mild amusement, that the truth requires not the right information but simply the correct perspective.

'Nobody would have guessed he was that kind of man,' Evelyn says, digging into a bag of raisins. 'I mean, such a controlling man. Such a cruel man. You couldn't tell from the outside.'

'Cruel?' Rebekah says.

'Lilly had no idea until they were married.'

Rebekah notices her own figure reflected in Evelyn's sunglasses—a sprawled-out woman in a fuchsia bikini, overshadowed by Sebastian's outline.

'Of course by then it was too late. She felt she had to stick with him. God, the things she put up with. Sultanas?'

Evelyn is offering the bag. Rebekah isn't fond of raisins, least of all fat ones like these which remind her of flies whose wings have fallen off. She pinches out a cluster anyway, feeling obliged, and reaches back to Sebastian.

'Want some?' she says.

Her fingers brush against his palm. Evelyn is gazing off at the children: 'David, Kate, are you hungry?'

The children ignore her. They're at the shoreline with Muller, chucking wigs of seaweed into the water. An iceberg floats in the distance, majestic and lonely against the open horizon.

'Gorgeous day,' Rebekah says.

'It is,' Evelyn says, and she calls out louder: '*Are you hungry?*'

Sebastian brushes her thigh again. A blade of grass, yes, or something like it, although what she senses isn't the grass itself but Sebastian's fingers pinched around the stalk, and Sebastian's hand leading up to his arm, and his shoulder, and his handsome head—what she perceives, in fact, is the silky brush of Sebastian's mind tracing itself over her skin. Her goose pimples are rising, tiny volcanoes of thrill, erupting everywhere.

'David! Kate!'

The children are running off. Muller jogs after them, waving reassurances. Evelyn gives a sigh, smiling, and turns to Rebekah.

'Is she all right now?' Rebekah says. 'Your sister.'

'Lilly's fine, I suppose. It took her years to stop blaming herself. She thought everything was her fault—even when he tried to kidnap the children.'

'Kidnap? Are you serious?'

'He tried to take them back to Dubai. The police caught him as they were boarding the plane. A matter of minutes and they would have gotten away.'

'It wasn't kidnapping from his point of view,' Sebastian says. He traces the blade of grass higher, nudging Rebekah's bum. Ripples of pleasure spread through her belly and across the sand and the water and the ribs of the clouds. The earth is shivering at Sebastian's touch. Evelyn fingers the raisins, probing something with a frown. Rebekah scissors her legs apart a little, inviting Sebastian to carry on, to take it further, to risk getting caught.

To risk—to explode the truth.

She imagines it, the exploded truth, splattered over the beach. Everybody dripping in the ugly truth.

'It was culturally reasonable from his point of view,' Sebastian says.

'A hair,' Evelyn says. She plucks it from the bag and holds it before her. 'Disgusting.'

'Yuck,' Rebekah says.

'Wait, it's only David's.' She lifts up her sunglasses and inspects the specimen. 'Yes, it's his colour. Thank goodness. And I thought it was a rat's.' She aims her grey eyes at Rebekah, and then at Sebastian: 'How could it be reasonable from any point of view? I mean, *really*. It was pathological.' She flicks away the hair and pulls down her glasses.

Muller and the children are at the other end of the beach, clambering up a sandy slope.

'Who's coming for a swim?' Sebastian says.

Rebekah notices his shadow rising to its feet. He peels off a shadowy T-shirt and casts it aside. He walks toward the shore and for a moment both women are watching him: the thick shoulders and back, the Rodin musculature. A man carved from rock.

He strides into the water.

'It must be freezing,' Evelyn says.

Rebekah reaches back and finds the thing that was brushing her. It's not a blade of grass but something thicker, like a thread, as if from a rope.

Was it only the wind moving the thread?

It must have been.

Affairs happen mostly in the imagination. It's the harsh reality she tries to ignore.

Affair—in the past she would never have used that word

to refer to herself and Sebastian. But the bland, seedy term is somehow fitting now, if still utterly distasteful.

Sebastian wades up to the waist. He dives in and starts swimming.

Rebekah looks down the beach and sees Muller and David at the top of the sandy slope. They're squatting under a plateau of grass that's jutting over them like a toupee. Muller and the boy wave, and the women wave back.

'Sometimes I think I've got Lilly's problem,' Evelyn says.

'What problem is that?'

'I'm too passive. And the worst thing is it can be so easy, like a mental surrender. Rather than standing up for yourself, you roll over.'

Rebekah digs her toes into the hot sand. 'I suppose I get that way too sometimes. It's normal, isn't it?'

'I wouldn't call it normal. Not at all. It makes me quite angry, in fact. It makes me feel as if—oh look, here they go now.'

Muller is bounding down the slope with David on his back. They tumble into a pile of sand.

'He's so good with the children,' Evelyn says.

'He is,' Rebekah says, glancing toward the bay. Sebastian is swimming straight out toward the iceberg. A bluish-white mountain, haloed by a whirl of gulls.

'What I meant to say—' Evelyn says.

'Hmm?'

'—is that it makes me feel as if I could scratch out someone's eyes.'

She turns to Evelyn. The sun has brought out the age

in her face. The brackets around her faintly curled lips, the wrinkles stitched about her neckline.

'That's what happens,' Evelyn says. 'When I get angry. When I feel like someone has pushed me too far—or if someone has crossed me. You must know the feeling?'

'Yes. I think I do.'

Evelyn reaches into the raisin bag. Something brushes the back of Rebekah's thigh. The wind and a thread. Her cruel imagination.

'More sultanas?'

'I've got some, thanks.'

'Yes I see—in your hand. You must have squished them to death by now.'

Rebekah opens her fist and looks at them. A clump of fat flies. She pops them into her mouth and swallows them together.

'Gorgeous day,' Evelyn says. 'Isn't it?'

Evelyn knows something. She's hinting, sending a warning. There's no other explanation for it.

That night at the rental cabin Rebekah hears a door slam. She stares into the bathroom mirror, her mouth frothing with toothpaste. Are they fighting? Is there going to be a scene?

She rinses her mouth and listens. She opens the door a crack.

Silence.

She finishes up and crosses the hallway to the guest room that she and Muller are using. He's sitting on the bed, hunched with his arms around his knees, deep in thought. A novel is propped open beside him.

'Bek?' he says as she begins searching through her travel bag.

'What.'

'I wanted to talk to you.'

'About what?'

'I just, uh.'

She looks at him. 'Talk to me about what? What is it?'

'I don't think I've always been faithful to you.'

'What?'

'I mean—'

'What are you saying?'

'Alright. I haven't been—I haven't been faithful to you.'

'Are you saying you've—?'

'No. Not really.'

'It's either yes or no, Mull.'

'It's no. But in my heart, you know. I've been unfaithful.'

'What is that supposed to mean?'

'I mean I have fantasies. Sometimes. About other women.'

'Fantasies?' she laughs. 'Are you saying you masturbate?'

'That's not what I meant. The point is—'

'Will you please just *say* it?'

'The point is, I don't feel good about it. I mean the fantasies.'

She laughs, digging into the bag. She finds her long nightshirt.

'It isn't funny, Bek.'

'It *is* funny. I mean, is that what you're sitting here brooding about? Sometimes I just don't understand how you see things.' She undresses and slips the shirt on. 'Why did you leave the window open? The bugs are getting in.'

She goes to the window and tries to slide it down.

There's a soft rap at the door.

Muller gets up and opens it. 'Pardon me,' Sebastian says. 'Were you finished in the bathroom? I think Rebekah left her toiletries.'

'Sorry,' she says.

She slips between the two men and crosses the hall. Her toiletry bag is open on the sink. She pretends to look for something inside it, and Sebastian comes up behind her and she turns. 'Everything okay?' she whispers.

'She's got a migraine.'

'Can we still go for a walk tomorrow—with the kids?'

'I don't think so. It could last for days.'

She stares at him. She can never tell if he's lying. She goes back to the room and closes the door. She walks to the window.

'Bek,' Muller says. 'Will you listen? I wanted to say I'm sorry.'

'Sorry about what?'

'What I just mentioned.'

'God, Mull, why do you dwell on these things? It's no big deal. Doesn't the average guy think about sex every seven seconds?'

'This isn't about the average guy. It's about me.'

'This thing is jammed.'

'I'm trying to admit something to you.'

'Then *admit* it.'

'The girl at the convenience store, for example.'

'Which girl?'

'Well, she's sort of buxom.'

'The ice cream girl?'

'Yes. And it seems to me that if I'm looking at her and imagining things with her—'

'Imagining what? She's naked and covered in gelato?'

'Exactly,' Muller laughs awkwardly. 'That sort of thing.'

'Can you try this?'

He comes over. He presses down on the window frame, and after a moment it gives, shutting with a bump. 'There. Will you listen now?'

She returns to her bag. 'Everyone has thoughts about other people, Mull.' She pulls out a pair of three-quarter length pants.

He touches her shoulder.

'God!' she says. 'You scared the hell—'

'Listen to me, Bek.'

'*What.*'

'There was a woman at work.'

'A woman.'

'Yes.'

'You had an affair?'

'No! It wasn't that.'

'Then what. Will you please *say* it?'

'She was sort of pretty and—again, it was distracting. Like the ice cream girl.'

'So do you talk to her?'

'The one at work?'

'Yeah.'

'That was a long time ago. She moved to a different part of the building. Anyway, it's not like anything happened. She was just another, you know. Fantasy.'

You had an affair, she thinks.

It's a relief.

She walks to the closet. She grabs a shirt sleeve and presses it to her nose. 'Everything smells like linoleum in here.'

'Why do you walk away like that?'

'Because I hate it when you talk this way.'

'I'm only trying to explain myself.'

'I need to hang these someplace where it doesn't stink.'

'Can we put the pants aside for a second? Please?' He pulls them out of her hands and tosses them onto the bed.

'What do you want, Mull?'

'I'm trying to tell you I feel badly.'

'I *get* it—you're guilty. Now can I have my pants?'

'It's not just a feeling. It's like we've drifted apart—like *I've* drifted away from you. That's what I'm trying to tell you. I want to be closer to you again.'

'Fine. Then treat me like you mean it—and stop focusing on your guilt.'

'Why are you so upset?'

'I'm not upset. I just hate it when you're so guilty.'

'I can't help it sometimes. It's like—'

'I know what it's like. You've told me before. You've got a

policeman in your head. You get infractions for every little mistake. I'm tired, Mull. Can I have my pants?'

He steps aside and she sees them on the bed. The legs are spread invitingly wide. She snatches them and goes to a small table.

She lays the pants down, and starts sweeping away the creases, and hears a cry across the hall. One of the children is waking. It sounds like Kate. The cry grows louder—a door is opening—and then Rebekah catches Sebastian's voice, tender and soothing.

She runs her hand across the creases, and waits until everything is quiet. 'Mull?' she says.

'What.'

'I want to be closer too. I just don't like it when you're so guilty.'

'I know.'

'Don't apologize anymore. Alright? Whatever you do.'

She braces herself for the rest of the weekend. She fears an open accusation from Evelyn, an ugly scene, but the moment never comes. The only sign is a chill wafting from the woman, as if she herself has become the iceberg on the horizon, carrying a cold breeze.

Rebekah doesn't mention anything to Sebastian. She doesn't want to trouble him. Maybe he already knows? Maybe he and Evelyn have fought about it? Maybe Evelyn is the sort of wife who tolerates her husband's mistress, and even appreciates that she occasionally babysits their children? The height of civility: politeness at all costs.

The summer fades into autumn, and still nothing happens, except that she develops a quiet hatred for Evelyn. Hates the politeness and the paisley shawls. Hates that she chews food with her lips pinned. Hates everything about the woman—and the feeling never quite settles except when Rebekah is in Sebastian's arms, sprawled on his two-seater couch.

Then, she might even feel some pity for Evelyn. But the feeling never lasts long, and she never really regrets her involvement with Sebastian. It might be an 'affair', but it was never meant to hurt Evelyn or anybody. In fact, Rebekah has always been inclined to believe that the affair strengthens the Ashfields' marriage—not to mention Rebekah's own marriage. Sebastian himself once claimed that the most stable relationship arrangement, at least among 'mature couples', was not a marriage, but a marriage with a lover on the side. He cited various proofs, mostly from French politics and modern novels, although the greatest proof, for Rebekah, was and still is the simple fact that she and Sebastian have something special, something that completes and fulfills each of them. If their relationship has such a positive effect on their own lives, then surely it must benefit the lives of the people around them?

As long as those people don't know about it.

Of course she senses she's fooling herself, repeating old stories that she used to really believe, like a person who still finds comfort in a church long after her faith has mostly slipped away. What she can no longer deny is that Sebastian has changed. He's become more distant, and there's a machine-like tedium to his movements when they make love. The change, it seems, began when he returned from Europe and cut her off after she brought up Paris—although she admits he may have already started to emotionally withdraw even before she left for the pilgrimage.

It's only natural, she supposes, that feelings wear off over time, but she can't help worrying that he's getting tired of her. Bored of her.

Or has he decided she's not good enough for him— lacking, perhaps, in some quality of character? Maybe he's begun to compare her to Evelyn, and found her, Rebekah, to be *wanting*?

The worries gnaw at her. They run about her mind like rats in the dark.

'It was nice to be with you,' she says one day, after the sex.

His head is resting on her belly. Has he dozed off?

'What are you reading these days?' she says.

'What?'

'Are you reading anything?'

'*Love in the Time of Cholera*.'

'I thought you read that last year.'

'I'm reading it again.'

A fibre in the couch is prodding her hip. She shifts, slightly, trying not to discomfort him. 'I'm reading T.S. Eliot. Muller gave me the collected poems for my birthday. He always gives me things that he would have given himself.'

'T.S. Eliot is fine, as long as you read before 1927.'

'Why 1927?'

'His best years were then. After 1927 he was essentially a moralist.'

'I didn't know that. That's interesting.' She runs a finger over the back of his neck. 'Can I ask you something.'

'What.'

'How did you meet Evelyn?'

'What are you really asking, Rebekah?'

She becomes still, her palm flattened against the crocodile lumps of his spine. 'I feel like she'll always be more important to you. No matter what happens.'

'You're probably right about that.'

She waits, but he doesn't say anything more. He's not even annoyed with her.

Doesn't he care enough to get annoyed? Doesn't he see that she's hurting?

She walks home later that afternoon. She climbs the stairs of the apartment, takes off her boots, and looks in the mirror. Her hair is flecked with glittering snowflakes. She's prettier than Evelyn, and younger by a decade, but it's the inside that matters, isn't it? That's what makes the difference between the woman he loves and the woman he screws. The brains, the maturity, the damn civility.

'How was your day?'

She sees Muller in the mirror, over her shoulder. He's in track pants and a shapeless yellow sweatshirt. It's his day off.

'Fine,' she says. She walks over and gives him a peck.

'Can we sit down?' he says.

'Why?'

'Come with me. We need to talk.'

He takes her hand and leads her into the kitchen.

'What's wrong?' she says. 'What's going on?'

'Nothing's wrong. Sit down.' He tugs his chair closer and holds her hands on his knees. 'I've been thinking,' he says. 'I think we should have a baby.'

'A baby?'

'I know we used to talk about it. I know I was the one who wanted to put it off. I think the time is right, now.'

Yeats saunters into the room. He weaves through Rebekah's ankles.

She looks at him and looks at Muller. 'You want to have a baby.'

'You seem surprised.'

'I'm wondering why now all of a sudden?'

'I suppose I realized there was no use in waiting. We're married. We need to get on with our lives. Right?'

'I guess.'

'Don't you want a baby?'

'Well—I just haven't thought about it in so long.'

'I know. Because I made you wait. I shouldn't have done that.'

'But why is this occurring to you now?'

'I don't know why, Bek. I guess I want us to be closer. You seem annoyed or something.'

'I'm not annoyed. It's just so sudden.'

'We've been married over a year and a half. Don't you think it's time?'

'Are you really ready for a baby?'

'I *am* ready. That's why I'm bringing it up.'

'What about your writing? Didn't you want to finish a novel, or a book of poetry?'

'I can always write. Anyway, there are more important things in life.'

The snowflakes in her hair have melted to droplets. They're creeping over her scalp like ants.

'What is it?' he says, confused by the silence.

'I don't know,' she laughs.

'Don't you want one?'

'Of course I do. I'm just not used to you talking like this.'

All her life she's envisioned herself as a mother. A real natural—the kind who breastfeeds in cafés and carries her baby in a cloth sling with vibrant African patterns. But does she want to have a baby with Muller? At least a part of her does: the part that's still fond of him, that believes he'll make a good father. She can love Muller's baby while only half-loving Muller.

The question is how Sebastian will react. He might be jealous—or he might lose interest. She isn't sure how to bring it up.

One night she and Muller are at the Ashfields' house. Evelyn takes a sip of wine. 'This is nice,' she says. 'Very dark and earthy.'

'With hints of chocolate,' Sebastian says, twirling his glass. 'Did you notice the tannins?'

Rebekah slides her foot forward beneath the table. Eyeing him over the rim of her glass, she pivots her foot left and right like a periscope. They don't play footsies anymore but she still nudges him on occasion, hoping for a response. A comforting stroke.

'So when did you guys decide to have kids?' Muller says.

Rebekah stiffens.

'I was only wondering, you know. Was it something you'd planned all along, or was it—? Did it just—?'

Muller gives a chuckle, as if realizing the awkwardness of the question.

Evelyn, true to form, receives his inquiry politely. 'We always intended to have a family,' she says. 'We delayed like most people, I suppose, although I do remember feeling that something was missing. I think we both felt it,' she says, turning to Sebastian.

He makes a slight noise from his throat.

'I recall one day,' she continues. 'It was our ninth anniversary, and we were sitting in a restaurant by a large mirror. I remember seeing us in the mirror, just the two of us, and feeling as if—'

'As if you were incomplete?' Muller says.

'No. Not incomplete. *Insubstantial.* That's the word. As if we needed more substance, more emotional weight. We're emotional beings, after all. We've evolved to take on that weight. Sebastian, does that make sense?'

'Certainly, yes.'

'And now that you have children, do you feel emotionally heavier?' Muller says.

'I feel rather obese, to be honest,' she says with a smile. 'Sometimes I wish I could trim down again.'

Everybody laughs.

Muller looks at Rebekah. 'Shall we tell them? If it's okay with you.'

'Tell us what?' Evelyn says. 'Are you expecting?'

'No, no,' they say together.

'Not yet anyway,' Muller says. 'But we've decided, you know, to gain some weight. Emotional weight.'

She can't believe he brought it up. She wasn't ready for this. The couples raise their glasses and toast to the news, but the Ashfields don't pester Muller and Rebekah with any more questions. They sense Rebekah's discomfort, or so she guesses, and the conversation discreetly turns to other subjects.

After supper they move their chairs to the windows. A snowstorm is sweeping across the coast, dulling the city's lights to a flicker. Rebekah watches Sebastian's reflection in the glass and keeps guessing at his feelings. Either he's hiding his reaction or he doesn't care. She finds herself alternately anxious and hurt—and alone. Cut off from him.

Near midnight Evelyn goes down to check on the children. A few minutes later she comes back up the steps and calls over: 'You must come see this. The door is blocked with snow.'

They head down to the entry. She opens the door and reveals a wall of white, waist high, stamped with the door's elegant moulding. The street beyond is a swirl of dunes, the vehicles half buried like relics in a desert. The snow is still coming down hard.

'It seems we'll have to dig our way out,' Muller says.

Evelyn pushes the door shut, squinting against the wind.

'It's late to be shovelling,' Sebastian says. 'Listen, why don't the two of you spend the night? The couch has a pull-out.'

Evelyn tilts her head at the suggestion.

'We wouldn't want to impose,' Muller says, glancing at Rebekah.

'No, of course not,' she says.

'It's really no trouble,' Sebastian says.

'Not at all,' Evelyn adds neutrally. 'The children will be thrilled to find you here in the morning.'

They go back upstairs and finish their drinks. They tidy up the living room and Sebastian pulls out the bed. Evelyn brings pillows and pyjamas and lays out fresh sheets.

'Why did you tell them?' Rebekah says after the Ashfields have gone.

'What?' Muller says. 'That we're trying?'

'You shouldn't have told them.'

'What's the big deal?'

'I'd rather keep it to ourselves. Until there's news. And I don't like being reminded that I'm going to gain weight.'

'I said *emotional* weight, Bek.'

She watches him put on the pyjamas. They're Sebastian's, cream with blue stripes. 'Look at me,' he says. 'I look like a convict.'

She turns to the window and gazes into the storm. At least Sebastian knows. It unnerves her, but at least he knows.

'You okay?' Muller says.

'It's all the snow. Makes me claustrophobic.'

He puts his arm around her and she catches the scent of the pyjamas. The spice of Sebastian's cologne.

She shoulders Muller away.

'What's the matter?' he says.

'I'm a bit uncomfortable. The snow.'

'But I'm not the snow. I'm *me*.'

'You know what I mean.'

'No, I don't. The snow is out there and I'm in here. If the snow is making you uncomfortable, then putting my arm around you shouldn't irritate you. It should help you.'

'It doesn't help me when you analyze me like that.'

Muller sighs irritably. He climbs onto the mattress and pulls up the blanket. 'By the way, I noticed you were drinking tonight. You should probably cut out the alcohol.'

'Why?'

'Because we're trying to get pregnant.'

'I'm not pregnant *yet*. I just finished my period—I was wearing pads until yesterday.'

'Sperm can survive for five days.'

'I don't ovulate until day fourteen. Do the math.'

'Why are you so touchy?'

'Because I *can't* get pregnant right now.'

'It's the principle of the thing, Bek. If we're trying to get pregnant then you shouldn't drink.'

'So *we're* getting pregnant, but *I'm* the one who shouldn't drink?'

'Bek.'

'How very logical, Muller.'

'You *know* what I'm saying.'

'Don't tell me what to do. Please. If you don't mind.'

He folds his hands behind his head and stares coldly at the ceiling. She takes Evelyn's T-shirt, then tosses it aside, preferring to sleep in her own blouse and underwear.

She slips out of her pants and turns off the lamp, and gets into bed. Foghorns are moaning in the distance. The two of them are going to be up for a while—she knows it. They both do. There'll be more talk, and more hurt, and then weary apologies, first him and then her.

That's their pattern, the karmic wheel of their relationship. Hurt and apology. Forever turning.

The wind is whistling when she wakens in the dark. She instantly thinks back to supper with dread—the look on Sebastian's face when Muller broke the news. A look she can never interpret, like the face of a portrait. The unblinking eyes.

She turns toward the window. The gales are raising ghosts off the snowy rooftops across the lane. No matter how Sebastian might feel, she knows that a baby will strengthen her—and she takes comfort in that. A baby will give her another place to anchor herself. Free her from her need for Sebastian.

She needs that, another anchor, another centre for her emotions and thoughts.

As she rolls onto her back again, she notices her bladder is full, and then recalls her conversation with Muller about alcohol. They managed to have a decent discussion in the end. For his part, he agreed that there was no harm in having a drink while she was on her period. For her part, she promised not to drink at any other times, although she privately resolved that she'd allow herself a sip whenever she felt like it—if only because Sebastian had once mentioned that a mere sip wouldn't harm a growing fetus.

Sebastian: here he is again, at the centre of everything.

She peels off the blanket and gets out of bed. The floor-boards are cold. She crosses through the dark kitchen, catching the lingering odour of supper, the thick smell of beef and fried onion, and starts down the steps. They're narrow and wooden, curving like a castle stairway, and she keeps her feet near the edges to avoid creaking.

The Ashfields' bedroom is at the bottom, on the ground floor—an odd design for a house, like so many houses in this old city. Their door is conveniently ajar. She pauses, and looks, but sees only the corner of the bed through the darkness. There's no snoring, no sound at all.

They're well-mannered even when they sleep.

She crosses the entry and passes the children's room. The night light in the bathroom is on, glowing over a cluster of lotion bottles.

She enters and closes the door softly. She sits down on the toilet and pees. A mobile over the counter, a flock of wooden birds, wavers in the air currents that she's brought in. She flushes and rinses her hands in the sink. She wipes them on a hanging towel and hesitates, looks in the mirror. She hooks her fingers underneath it and pops open the medicine cabinet.

An electric shaver. Hair gel. A bottle of pills. She takes

the bottle and turns the label toward her. The prescription is for Evelyn.

Rebekah has seen it before, discovered it one night while babysitting the children. She used to believe that Evelyn was too strong to become depressed, but apparently not. Apparently she's struggling. A faint smile creeps into Rebekah's lips as she turns the bottle, watching the capsules tumble over each other.

The door clicks and opens. It's Sebastian.

'What are you doing?' he says.

'I was just. Looking.' She puts the bottle on the shelf.

He shuts the door behind him. He moves toward her. 'Why didn't you tell me. That you're planning to have a baby.'

'I meant to. I was going to.'

'You make me feel as if I can't trust you.'

'Of course you can.'

'Keep your voice down.'

'You can always trust me. *Always.*'

'Then I need to know that you'll be open with me, Rebekah.'

'I was going to tell you. I didn't want to upset you.'

'I'm not upset about your decision. I'm upset you weren't open about it. That I had to find out like this. Out of the blue.'

'I'm *sorry.*'

'And what does this mean for us as a couple?'

A couple? He's never called them that before. 'It doesn't have to mean anything.'

'When did you decide?'

'A few days ago. He used to want to wait and now suddenly he wants one.'

'And what about you? Do you want one?'

'Yes, but it doesn't have to change anything between us. I don't want it to change anything.'

'You should have told me, Rebekah.'

'It won't happen again. I promise—I swear to you.'

He watches her. 'Come here,' he says. She moves toward him and he takes her into his arms. 'I care about you very much,' he says, stroking her hair. 'I want you to know that.'

'I didn't want to hurt you.'

'You haven't hurt me, Rebekah. I'm glad for you. I just don't want any secrets between us.'

He slips his hands under her blouse. 'It feels so good to be with you,' she says, tightening her arms around him. 'I don't ever want to lose you.'

'And you won't. We'll always be together.' He kisses her tenderly. His breath smells of toothpaste and cigar. 'Now I must be honest with you about something,' he whispers against her lips. 'Although I'm not sure I should tell you.'

She nibbles at him. 'Tell me. Come on.'

'It's just that when Muller said what he said, I was jealous. I even found myself wishing—I know it's mad—I wished I could have a baby with you too.'

She lowers her eyes.

'Maybe I shouldn't have said that. It was just a wish. I've always wanted a special bond with you.'

She stares into his chest. The floor is vibrating, as if from a distant earthquake.

'Don't fault me for imagining something deeper, Rebekah.'

She realizes it's the ploughs. They're roaring through the streets, peeling up snow and ice.

'Haven't you ever wished for something deeper?'

He touches her chin and everything is trembling.

'Yeah,' she whispers, looking up.

'I'm glad I could share this with you. I'm glad we can still be open with each other. I don't want us to lose that. Now you need to go back to bed. We must be quiet.'

He kisses the tip of her nose. She slips out of the bathroom and through the entry. She goes up the stairway, keeping her feet to the edges. She walks through the kitchen and sees Muller on the pull-out.

He's buried under the blanket, vague as a corpse.

PART THREE

REBEKAH IS PREGNANT BY APRIL. That summer Sebastian accepts a new job in Switzerland. He's going to manage the employee counselling program of an international firm.

The decision comes as a surprise to Muller. He assumed the Ashfields were content here, in this foggy town by the sea. He supposed the weekend suppers and cigarillos and pleasant conversation would continue indefinitely, and that the Ashfield children would grow up with his and Rebekah's boy—a boy, according to the ultrasound.

If there's any consolation, it's a series of delays that pushes the moving date into December. On their last night in the country the Ashfields come to Muller and Rebekah's place for supper. 'I thought we should drink this before you left,' Rebekah says, placing a bottle of red wine on the table. 'You served it the first time we had supper together.'

Sebastian studies the label. 'Yes, our favourite *Rioja*. Quite fitting.' He takes the corkscrew and presses it into the bottle.

'Wait,' Muller says. 'Before you open it I wanted to say a few words—if I may.'

Sebastian regards him a moment, then puts down the corkscrew. Evelyn gives an approving nod.

'I wanted to say—'

'Is this a toast?' Rebekah says. 'Because if it's a toast then we should open the bottle.'

'I suppose it could be a toast. It doesn't really matter. I only wanted to say—'

'Then we should open the bottle.'

'Let me speak. Please. All I wanted to say, Sebastian, Evelyn, is that we'll miss you guys. We'll miss you and the children and the friendship we've all shared. When I think back to the day we met—'

'Look!' Kate cries. 'Look, look!'

'What is it?' Evelyn says.

The girl is pointing at the Christmas tree. 'I want the princess—the princess up there.'

'That's not a princess, that's an angel. An imaginary being.'

'She looks so pretty.'

'But angels aren't real,' David mutters. 'They're made-up things.'

'Actually, they're a *symbol*,' Muller says.

'Nooooo!' David says, rolling his eyes. 'They're not a *symbol*!'

'I want the symbol, I want the symbol!' Kate cries.

Muller climbs onto a chair and takes down the angel for her. The girl hugs it affectionately, and then David insists on something too, and so Muller strips off a few more ornaments—shiny balls, nutcracker soldiers, threads of tinsel—which the children divide between them. By the time Muller returns to the table Sebastian is pouring the wine.

'Cherries,' Evelyn says, sniffing her glass.

'Black cherries,' Sebastian says.

'And there's something else here too. Tobacco, I think.'

Everybody drinks but Rebekah. She's nine months pregnant and toasts with mineral water.

'Do they wonder about the holiday?' Muller says, watching the children. 'What it all means? The trees and decorations.'

'You ask that every year,' Rebekah says.

'Do I?'

'Every year. The same question.'

'We say it's a time to be with family,' Evelyn says. 'They understand that some people are religious, but they know that we aren't.'

Muller looks at Rebekah. 'What are we going to tell our little boy when he starts to ask?'

'Tell him what you think,' Evelyn says.

'But I'm not sure what I think. I suppose I believe in something. Not in religion, but something. A vague something.'

Evelyn raises her glass. 'A toast to a vague something, then.'

'Yes, a toast,' Muller says. 'Because a vague something is better than a complete nothing.'

'Even if there is only nothing.'

They laugh and drink.

'Of course, there must be *something*,' he says, gesturing at the ceiling. 'I mean up there. Otherwise everything is just chance. Just physical matter.'

'Why *just* chance?' Evelyn says. 'Why *just* matter?'

'Isn't it obvious? I mean, if everything in the universe exists purely because of chance, then everything is pointless.'

'A universe of chance is still a marvellous place.'

'Marvellous, but ultimately dead.'

'Dead but ultimately marvellous,' Sebastian says.

Rebekah laughs. Muller feels a spark of irritation but smiles, containing himself. 'Think about it logically,' he says. 'If the universe really *is* just a product of chance, then nothing can truly mean anything. It's all a pointless accident. The universe. This room. This conversation. But if the universe is a result of some kind of design rather than chance, if there's really a God—'

Rebekah shoots a weary glance at him.

'A couple of years ago I had a patient,' he says. 'A young man. A talented pianist. The next Bach, they said, the next Chopin.'

'Is this necessary?' Rebekah says.

'Let me speak. This patient—we'll call him Richard—he suffered a brain haemorrhage. It left him paralyzed so that he couldn't move his hands anymore. Just a little.' Muller lifts his hands off the table and wiggles the fingers. 'Not even that much.'

'Dreadful,' Evelyn says.

'He became depressed. He wanted to die. Then he had a dream in which he found himself seated before a piano, in a packed concert hall. There was a sheet of music in front of him and he was expected to play, but knew he couldn't, so he just sat there, unsure of what to do. The audience began booing, and people began walking out of the concert hall until, at last, there was only one person left. To his horror, Richard realized it was the composer of the music. The composer was waiting to hear what he'd written. Richard stared at the music sheet, feeling more and more helpless. Then he had a peculiar thought: *The music is real, even if I can't play it. The music exists, even if there's nobody to hear it.* At that moment, the composer began clapping, and the sound of a beautiful piano concerto began filling up the hall. You see? The music was real. Nobody was playing it—nobody that Richard could see—and yet it was there, present. It was the most wonderful music he'd ever heard, and then he *knew*. You see? He *knew*.'

'Knew what?' Evelyn says.

'He knew the composer was God. God was telling him, *There is meaning in the world, even if you don't see it. There is a true and beautiful reality, even if you don't believe it. This reality doesn't depend on your feelings and perceptions for its existence—it's there, independent of you, because I, God, created it.*'

Rebekah gets up with a huff. She begins collecting the plates. Sebastian is gazing at the children with a ruffled brow.

'So what happened to Richard?' Evelyn says.

'The dream was so powerful, left such an impression on him, that it triggered a spiritual conversion. He asked to see the hospital chaplain and was baptized. His depression began to lift. He told me, in one of our last conversations, that he believed there was something to live for now. He was convinced his life had some kind of purpose, even if he couldn't play music again. Unfortunately, a few weeks later—'

Rebekah drops some cutlery onto a plate. Muller winces at the clatter, then gives a difficult smile.

'He died. A pulmonary embolism. But I believe he died peacefully. Excuse me.'

He follows Rebekah to the kitchen. 'What is the matter?' he says.

'Did you have to bring that up?'

'Why shouldn't I?'

'It's a morbid story. The children were listening.'

'They weren't listening.'

'It's their last night here, Mull.' She dumps the plates into the sink. 'We don't need to talk about morbid things.' She runs the faucet and rinses her hands.

'You always oppose me,' he says.

'When do I oppose you?'

'When I try to make a point—you never agree. And it wasn't a morbid story.'

'He died.'

'He died *peacefully*.'

She brushes past him, and her belly bumps against his hip.

'Careful,' she snaps. 'There's a baby in there.'

Sebastian becomes oddly quieter. He seems to ignore

everything that Muller says, and Muller worries that Rebekah was right—it was a mistake to tell that story. He'd hoped to impress everybody with his insights, to entertain them, but he miscalculated to the point of being offensive.

They have lemon cake and tea for dessert. Sebastian takes the children upstairs so they can have a nap before the late night flight. Muller admits to himself that tonight isn't the first time Sebastian has ignored him. It's been happening for months. He can recall entire evenings when Sebastian barely looked him in the eye. He wonders, now, if he offended him in those instances as well—or merely bored him by rambling too much?

Not that there's much difference between being boring and offensive. Not for Sebastian. Being boring, the Englishman once remarked, is the only real sin in life.

'Are they asleep?' Evelyn says when he returns to the living room.

'Yes,' Sebastian smiles. 'Kate was so sweet. She wanted to know if Aunt Beky was coming with us.'

'*So sweet,*' Rebekah coos. She rubs a hand over her belly: 'Tell her we'll visit in the spring, and we'll bring along a little friend.'

'Oh, we'll definitely visit,' Muller says. 'We'll visit as often as we can—if you'll have us, of course.'

'Of course,' Evelyn says.

'Now why don't I boil another pot of tea, or we can break out the port? Sebastian, what do you think?'

Sebastian is looking at his watch. 'I should probably call the cab now.'

'Now?' Evelyn says. 'Are you sure it's not too early?'

'A cab?' Rebekah says.

'I'm going to check in the luggage ahead of time. That way the children can rest a bit longer. I'll call when I'm ready.'

Rebekah watches him with a hint of confusion, a hand still on her belly. 'But you don't need to call a cab,' Muller says. 'I could drive you to the airport.'

Sebastian declines with a mumble. He rises from his chair and heads to the kitchen to make the phone call, and fifteen minutes later he's gone. Muller and the women continue the conversation, although without Sebastian the mood becomes flat. As he glances across the table, at the empty cups and dessert plates and the half-drunken bottle of *Rioja*, Muller realizes that this is it—their final get-together, their last supper. And it's already over.

He wishes he never brought up that story. The tale of a dead man, of all things.

It's after ten thirty when Sebastian calls from the airport. They wake up the children and bring them down to the car. Muller drives quickly, eyeing the clock on the dashboard. The flight is at midnight and he hopes there might be time to chat with Sebastian and leave him, perhaps, with a better impression of the evening.

They proceed to the baggage counter first, where Sebastian promised to meet them. The zigzagging rope line is filled with travellers, but there's no sign of him.

After a few minutes they walk the length of the terminal and then back to the baggage counter. There's a waiting area nearby, and they settle into a row of chairs. Kate clings to her mother's arm. 'Where's Daddy? Where is he?'

'He'll be here in a moment, Katie,' Evelyn says.

The girl's eyes are rimmed with tears.

'I'll have another look around,' Muller says. 'I'm sure I'll find him.'

'I can come with you,' Rebekah says.

'No. Better that you stay here.'

He hurries off, not wanting her to tag along. If Sebastian is to be found then Muller wants the credit.

He heads back up the terminal and wanders into the executive lounge on the chance that Sebastian is enjoying a glass of Scotch. Muller doesn't see him among the mostly empty tables, and so he checks the pub next door, and then peeks under the stalls of the bathroom, still without luck. As he comes out, perplexed, he notices a fossil display in a glass case—brachiopods in a massive chunk of sandstone. They look like scallop shells, angled toward a nearby stairway that leads up to an observation deck.

Muller walks over and climbs the steps. As he reaches the top he sees a man and woman embracing in a corridor.

'Sebastian?'

His friend looks over, perfectly composed.

'We're here,' Muller says.

'Thanks, man. I'm on my way.'

Sebastian's arms are draped over the woman's shoulders as if he owns her. Her face is buried in his chest. Muller absorbs the scene like a needle injection.

He turns and heads down the stairs. He wanders past

travellers and luggage carts, knowing he can't say anything about what he's just witnessed. He doesn't want to cause any trouble. He doesn't want to hurt anybody. Of course, it's not the only reason.

Another man's secret reminds you of your own. That's closer to the truth.

He reaches the waiting area. He sees Evelyn and the children and Rebekah. They're watching him approach and the lie has already formed in his mind. A simple lie. A bundle of words. He feels the weight of it behind his eyes and notices the moon in the window, swollen almost to fullness, as if about to burst its cold light onto the city.

'Well?' Evelyn says. 'Did you find him?'

'He was on the observation deck—right up the stairs. He's on his way.'

'Is he coming, Mummy?' Kate says.

'Yes, Daddy's on his way.'

Sebastian shows up a minute later, poised as ever. The children run to him and tug at his jacket. There are no questions about why he wasn't at the baggage counter or what he was doing on the observation deck, but Muller isn't surprised. Nobody questions the man.

They gather up the carry-on bags. They walk to the escalator and check the Ashfields' flight on the overhead screens. The plane is boarding.

'Perhaps we'll see you in the spring,' Evelyn says.

'Yes,' Muller says. 'In the spring.'

They hug and say their goodbyes. 'All the best,' Muller whispers to Sebastian, patting his back as they exchange a rigid embrace. Your secret is safe with me—that's what Muller wants him to know.

It's safe, at least for the moment.

He doesn't mention anything to Rebekah on the drive home. He's still coming to grips with what he witnessed. He feels betrayed, betrayed on behalf of everybody, although he now understands why Sebastian was so quiet after supper. He was preoccupied with his rendezvous.

Cunning bastard.

For all that, Muller can't deny a sense of awe. Sebastian Ashfield is having an affair. Not the fumbling kind of liaison that Muller had with Lara three years ago, but a *real* affair surely, with regularly scheduled sex and well-managed secrecy. It's quite astonishing.

Muller finds himself torn between admiring the man and resenting him.

'It'll be nice to see them in the spring,' Rebekah says, later in bed.

'It will. Assuming the baby can travel.'

'What do you mean *assuming*?'

'We can't be sure until he arrives, right? Babies are unpredictable.'

'Of course he'll be able to travel. What are you talking about?'

'I'm only saying that some things aren't certain.'

'I don't like it when you talk like that.'

'Like what?'

'You assume the worst. You always see the negative.'

'I said that some things aren't certain, Bek. That's not negative. It's just a fact of life.'

She flicks off the lamp. They roll away from each other. The blanket stretches between them, tensing like a tug of war, and then relaxes.

He thinks about Lara. He remembers his first day at the hospital—that first gush of milky emotion. How easily it all comes back to him, like an instinct, a reflex. The yearning fills him, the memories pulse through him in warm colours.

Rebekah begins to snore. He waits a few minutes, wallowing in a pool of recollections, and then slips off to the bathroom to indulge himself.

To indulge: to masturbate. He does it every day. He usually invites Lara into his fantasies, although sometimes other women, depending on his mood. The pleasure is reliable but Muller has mixed feelings about the act. It's had a bad reputation historically, yet he tries, at times, to believe the latest theories, which claim that masturbation is really a method of self-discovery and exploration—in essence like writing poetry: solitary, imaginative, valuable to the soul. But he's never truly fooled. Nobody jerks off for the creative challenge.

He can see the stump of his penis in the dim light. How ugly it is, the penis. How uniquely, distinctively ugly, this faceless head with its wispy cap. Why did Nature make us this way? Why should an appendage the shape of bratwurst have anything to do with desire? An organ of desire ought to be attractive. It ought to be a work of art. The human sexual organs, with their leaky stenches and ridiculous hair and general misshapenness, couldn't be called 'attractive' by even the most generous definition of the word, and they certainly aren't the reason we fall in love. You don't see a woman's vagina and then fall in love with the woman. You don't see a man's penis and think, Hmm, he'll make a good husband. It's the beautiful parts of a person that attract us in the beginning—the face, the limbs, the curves of the body, to say nothing of the personality—it's *these* parts that convince us we want to spend our lives with another person. But then, for some inexplicable reason, we discover a passion for the grotesque parts. The waste holes. It makes no sense. Why can't we have sex through a pair of pretty blue eyes?

The thought gives Muller pause. He remembers Lara's eyes with a flash of disappointment.

No matter.

He finishes his business and goes back to bed.

A few days later, Muller and Rebekah are walking along a gentle cliff trail near the harbour. He isn't comfortable with her walking long distances while nine months pregnant, and certainly not up here on the cliffs, but walking is the only exercise she can get these days and she stubbornly insists on doing it with a view of the ocean.

They go slowly and he stays a few steps ahead of her, now and then kicking aside stones. They reach a tourist lookout on a high point of rock. The Atlantic is spread out before them, grey and uneasy in the wind gusts, shuddering like the skin of a cold animal. 'There's something I wanted to tell you,' he says.

'What is it?'

'About Sebastian. That night at the airport. I saw him with a woman.'

She turns to him. Her hair is whipping in the wind like the snakes of Medusa. 'A woman?' she says.

'I didn't see her face clearly. She was hugging him.'

'Hugging? You're sure?'

'They were hugging each other. It was a close hug. Too close.'

'My God.'

'Yeah, I know. I meant to tell you sooner, but—'

'And you didn't see her face?'

'Not really. But she was young, I think. She had dark hair. That's all I could really see. I didn't recognize her.'

'My God. Poor Evelyn.'

'And it goes to show, doesn't it? You think you know people. You think you can trust them.'

'Are you sure you saw things right?'

'Oh, I'm sure. I didn't say anything at the time because I didn't want to cause any trouble.'

'I can't believe he would do that to her.'

'It makes sense that he didn't want me to help with the luggage. Do you remember? He didn't want me to drive him to the airport.'

She turns to the ocean. Tides slam against the rocks and mist wafts up, speckling their faces.

'I don't think we ever really knew him,' Muller says. 'There was always something about him, something he wasn't showing. Didn't you ever get that feeling? Behind all the charm? He hardly ever talked about his personal life. His past.'

'It's just such a shock. I can't believe he'd do something like that.'

'We can't say anything to Evelyn, alright? I don't want to cause problems for them. It could ruin their marriage. It's none of our business.'

'I know. It's just—'

'It doesn't have to affect us.' Muller gives her belly a rub. 'Anyway, we have other things to think about.'

He takes a certain pleasure in Rebekah's dismay. He's blemished her image of Sebastian Ashfield—and it's probably good for her. She admires Sebastian too much, keeps him up on a pedestal. Muller feels justified in taking him down a notch.

Of course there's some pettiness in it. You never know how much you resent another person until you discover their dirty secret. It's like finding out they're made of glass and being handed a stone.

Rebekah seems preoccupied for a day or two, as if brooding on the revelation, but then her mood lifts. She phones him from the café one morning while he's writing.

'I'm at The Tin Cup,' she says. 'I've been having cramps for two hours.'

'Do we need to get you to the General?'

'I think it's still early, but we should probably get ready. Could you come and pick me up?'

He hurries out the door and gets into the car in a mild

panic. The baby is coming—everything is going to change. He speeds down the road and senses his old life, his old concerns, fluttering behind him like dry leaves.

Rebekah is waiting outside the café as he pulls up to the curb. She's grimacing with a hand on her belly.

'Did you call the midwife?' she says.

'Not yet.'

'You should have called her.'

'You said it wasn't time.'

'I said it wasn't time to go to the *General*.'

Don't argue with her, he thinks.

He speeds back home and helps her up to the bathroom. Yeats meows after them. Muller runs downstairs, almost tripping over the cat, and calls the midwife. She says she'll come right over. He hears a scream. He runs up to the bathroom. Rebekah is leaning over the counter half naked. Her maternity jeans are heaped on the floor.

'Are you okay?' Muller says.

'Get our things ready. Pack the food.'

'Is it time?'

'Yes it's time! Pack the food!'

'Food? But you can't eat during the labour.'

'For *after* the labour!'

She means her snacks. Right. He hurries down to the kitchen and fills a cloth bag with organic apples, packages of nuts, and dried mango slices.

He runs back up to the bathroom. She's sitting on the toilet seat, bent forward with her eyes squeezed shut. He notices a spot of blood on the linoleum.

'You're bleeding,' he says.

'I'm fine. Did you call?'

'Yes. A few minutes ago.'

'Is she coming?'

'Yes.'

She holds her belly, teeth clenched. He stares at the blood spot. Spotting is normal, he knows. He's read about it in the books.

'You should eat,' she mutters. 'Before we leave. And feed Yeats.'

'Are you okay?'

'Just *go!*'

He hurries back down to the kitchen. He fills the cat bowl, hands trembling, and spills kibble all over the floor. He goes to the fridge and pours himself a glass of milk and pulls a hard bagel out of the bread bag. He takes a bite, chews, and washes it down with a gulp of milk. Rebekah screams.

'Oh God.'

He runs upstairs.

She's still on the toilet. 'The contractions are getting stronger.' She lets out a groan. Hisses through her teeth.

'It's going to be okay,' he whispers. 'Everything's fine.'

'Eat,' she says.

'Okay.' He takes a bite of the bagel.

'Not *here*.'

'Sorry. Sorry.' He goes downstairs and stands at the bay window.

What if she dies?

Please God, no.

The midwife pulls up to the curb in a purple jeep. He dashes down to the front door. Her name is Judy. She wears a purple sweater and has a purple suitcase of supplies.

They hurry upstairs. She helps Rebekah off the toilet and leads her to the bedroom.

'Lie back,' Judy says.

'I can't.'

'You have to. I have to check you out.'

Rebekah eases back on the bed, whimpering, and spreads her thighs. Judy feels inside her with a latex glove.

'You're seven centimetres.' She looks at Muller: 'We have to get going. *Now*.'

He collects Rebekah's backpack of clothes and toiletries and the food bag. Judy helps her slip into a pair of track pants and then supports her on the way down to the car. Rebekah kneels on the front seat with her arms wrapped around the headrest.

'You need to sit,' Muller says.

'I can't sit,' she says.

'He's right,' Judy says. 'You need to sit.' She helps Rebekah turn around and fastens her seatbelt. Muller drives quickly to the General and drops them off at the main doors. He parks in the employee lot, then runs back to the building and takes the elevator to maternity. A nurse directs him to the triage room. Rebekah is bent over the examination table with her pants down. A female doctor is feeling inside of her.

'You're fully dilated. I can't feel the cervix.'

A nurse leads them to the birthing room. Rebekah leans over the end of the bed. Another nurse comes into the room and flicks on the lights.

'No,' Rebekah says. 'I want it dim.'

'We need some light.'

'Please,' Muller says. 'Leave it dim.'

The nurse shrugs and turns down the lights. There's a splash. He sees a puddle on the floor under Rebekah. Judy helps her onto the bed. She's on her hands and knees, bare-bottomed, and he thinks of Lara. She had a nicer bum than Rebekah. No denying that—not to mention the breasts.

Snap out of it, Mull. Focus.

Doctor Parsons arrives and quietly greets Rebekah. He nods to Judy and Muller. He takes a stool to the corner of the room and sits, watching with his arms folded, a hand pressed under his chin. He's officially in charge, but agreed to leave as much as possible to the midwife. That's how they wanted it. How Rebekah wanted it.

Muller counts the time between contractions. It's about a minute. Her cries are agonized, her face twisted.

Please don't die.

He imagines a coffin in a snowy field. A smaller coffin next to it, a crowd of people in winter coats, their breath steaming in the cold. A nurse comes to the side of the bed with a needle. 'We need to take some blood,' she tells Rebekah. 'Can you turn on your side, honey?'

'I can't.'

Doctor Parsons comes to the bed. 'Rebekah, we have to take blood. You'll have to turn on your side.'

She lets out a long groan as they shift her onto her hip. Judy whispers soothingly in her ear while the nurse ties a rubber band around her arm.

She presses the needle in.

Muller watches the blood filling the tube. 'Hurry up,' he tells the nurse.

'I can't go any faster,' she says.

He looks toward the shutters. A view of the hospital rooftop—gravel and ventilation shafts. He remembers the room were Evelyn stayed after giving birth to Kate. It faced a wooded hill. The autumn colours were like campfires.

'All done,' the nurse says. She pulls the needle out and leans over Rebekah. 'You've got to push from your stomach, honey.'

'Shut up!'

He touches the nurse's shoulder. 'Please.'

She purses her lips and leaves the room. The contractions slow down. He walks to the corner where Doctor Parsons has taken his place on the stool again, hand under chin, observing patiently. Muller stands there a minute, then walks back to the bed, then walks back to the corner. She's moaning, now, rather than crying out, and between contractions the moans become soft and fluttery, as if the pain is tickling. At times she's completely still and gazing through half-closed eyes, like someone under hypnosis. How long is she going to last without an epidural? She insisted on doing things naturally.

'How much time before the baby comes?' he whispers to Doctor Parsons.

'Thirty to forty-five minutes.'

The contractions soon begin to quicken. Muller realizes that he's forgotten the camera. She wanted pictures. She wanted to show them to Sebastian and Evelyn, although he doesn't like the idea. He doesn't want the Ashfields to see her naked—at least not Sebastian. They had squabbled about it.

He warns himself not to argue with her in the coming days. She's going to be stressed and exhausted. Judy waves him over. Rebekah is lying on her side, and Judy is holding up Rebekah's leg. Muller takes over, cradling the leg with both arms, and notices something protruding from inside of her. It looks like a hairy tongue.

'What is that?' he whispers to Judy.

'The head.'

He's amazed at his uncertainty, his ignorance. Rebekah reaches down and touches the scruffy mass. She gasps with astonishment and begins pushing harder, crying out savagely, her face crunched up.

The baby's head bulges further out with each contraction—it's like expelling a bowling ball through your vagina, she'll later tell him. Doctor Parsons comes over and slips on some gloves. He presses his fingers around the head and begins to wriggle it out. Muller catches a strong foul odour like the smell of undergrowth, as if the child is emerging from the earth itself. The head slips out and he sees the face. It's clean and glossy, like a damp clay sculpture.

'Paul,' Doctor Parsons says, glancing back at Muller. The doctor is wriggling the body free. Muller reaches out and the rest happens as planned: Doctor Parsons transfers the baby into Muller's hands, and Muller moves the warm creature onto Rebekah's belly.

She pulls up her T-shirt. The child gives a cry—a furious, lusty cry, just as Muller read in the books. He laughs and tears are streaming down his face.

'It's a boy,' the nurse says matter-of-factly.

Eliot, he thinks.

Doctor Parsons gives him a pair of scissors. He snips the umbilical cord with a shaking hand. Judy puts her fingers to the baby's lips, spreading them apart, and presses his mouth against Rebekah's nipple.

'So beautiful,' Rebekah whispers.

Muller strokes the boy's back. 'Eliot. Eliot.' Rebekah looks at Muller with a warm smile.

'Eliot,' Doctor Parsons says. 'Nice name. Don't get many Eliots these days.'

There's a clang.

The nurse has thrown something into the garbage bin.

'I want that,' Rebekah says.

Muller looks inside. A small stone is lying amid the bloody tissues and pads. 'This?' he says, taking it out.

'Yeah,' she says. 'It's mine.'

He's seen the stone before. It's grey and smooth with an oblong shape. She rubs it in her hand while reading her novels in the evening. He doesn't think much of it now, and passes it to her.

Eliot is examined and pronounced healthy. The Apgar scores are perfect. Muller and Rebekah spend six hours in the maternity unit and then decide to take Eliot home rather than staying overnight at the hospital.

They lay him down on their bed. His closed eyes are like pinches of dough. Muller nudges the tiny fingers. 'I can't believe how cute he is. I think he looks more like you, Bek. The eyes, the mouth.'

'I can see a bit of you too.'

'Yeah?'

'The chin.'

'You think so?'

'Listen, I'm going to keep him in our bed tonight.'

'In *our* bed? What about the crib?'

'I'll have him on my chest. Skin-to-skin contact is good for newborns.'

'What if you roll over and crush him?'

'I won't crush him.'

'But you'll be asleep.'

'I'll be aware of everything.'

'What if he slips off you? What if *I* crush him?'

'You can sleep in the study.'

'In the study? You don't mind?'

'Not really. I mean, there's no point in both of us losing sleep.'

He takes two weeks off work. He cooks and cleans and does groceries, trying to be useful in this hurricane of change. Everything revolves around the baby. He's their little god, sacred and adored. Prone to fits of rage. Rebekah breastfeeds him on demand, day and night, and carries him about in a cloth sling. They hardly talk about anything but the boy—how he feeds, how he poops, how he sleeps, why he cries. Rebekah is irritable and tired, and pained by a tear in her vagina. They were told it could take weeks to heal. She says going to the bathroom is like peeing Tabasco sauce.

She shuffles into the study one morning, just as Muller is waking from a luxurious sleep. He sits up on his bed—a single mattress on the floor—and rubs his eyes and looks at her. Rebekah's pregnancy flab is hanging over the rim of her track pants. The flesh is marred with stretch marks, like the scars of bird claws.

'How was your night?' he says. 'I think I heard him crying.'

'I need some breakfast.'

'No problem.'

He goes down to the kitchen and prepares the usual for her—a glass of organic milk, bakery bread smeared with jam, and a bowl of pineapple slices.

He brings the food upstairs on a tray and finds her in the nursery. It's a spare room adjacent to the bedroom. Rebekah previously used it as an office, and it still has a desk and laptop. She's checking email.

'Any messages from Sebastian and Evelyn?' he asks.

'No. Nothing.'

He catches the annoyance in her voice. The Ashfields haven't communicated much since leaving.

'They must be busy,' Muller says. 'They're in a new country, starting new lives.'

'Still, you'd think.'

'We're in different worlds now. No point in hanging on.'

'I'm not *hanging on*.'

There's a whimper from the bedroom. Eliot begins to cry. Rebekah gives Muller a gloomy look and goes over to the boy. She ties him into the sling and begins swaying him from side to side.

The boy keeps crying.

Muller lingers in the doorway, too guilty to abandon her with a bawling infant. 'He usually likes being tied up, doesn't he?' he says.

'Usually,' she mutters.

'Maybe that's why adults like things tied up too? Mentally speaking, we don't like loose ends. Maybe infants express this in the need to be tightly swaddled? It's profound, sort of. When you think about it.'

'I'm not in the mood for this.'

'I'm only talking.'

'I'm *not* in the mood.'

Sitting down, Rebekah pulls up her shirt and holds Eliot to the breast, the right one—it's less bruised. He squirms and won't take it. She turns him about and tries the other breast. The welt on the nipple is like a purple tattoo.

Eliot clamps down on it. Rebekah sucks in her breath, suppressing the pain.

The boy lets go and starts wailing.

'Maybe we should check his temperature,' Muller says.

Rebekah takes the breast and presses it toward the boy's face. A stream of milk squirts through the air and speckles the carpet with droplets, like pearls.

'Let me take him, Bek. Please. I'll walk him around the house.'

She pushes him into Muller's arms. A shrieking bundle. Muller takes him into the nursery and starts circling the room. He jiggles him. He coos. He hops and lunges. The boy twists and screams hopelessly. Rebekah comes into the room. 'He doesn't have tears in his eyes,' Muller says. 'Is that normal?'

'Give him to me.'

She sits in the rocking chair. 'Shouldn't we check his temperature?' Muller says.

'He doesn't *have* a temperature. It's probably just gas.'

'Maybe something's poking him—maybe the diaper's too tight? Remember what Doctor Parsons said?'

'Would you please go away!'

Muller retreats to the study. Eliot cries on and off through the morning. He sleeps for a half hour in the afternoon and then starts wailing again. Rebekah and Muller take turns holding him. The boy howls and writhes, refusing to be consoled, raging against their every move—and yet, there are intervals when he goes silent for a few moments, eerily silent—and then he stares up from Muller's arms, his eyes hard and solemn, as if making a promise: a promise that there will be peace for a while. Peace and quiet and sleep. Then his face contracts, his body stiffens, and his gummy, milk-drenched mouth opens wide in a fit of shrieking.

Muller wants to slam him against the wall.

Darkness settles over the neighbourhood. Muller carries him downstairs and paces up and down the living room, clenching his jaw against the cries, against the aching in his back and arms.

He notices a photograph above the fireplace, under a gash of street light. A statue by Michelangelo. The *Dying Slave*. A classical male figure in a ravished pose—a hand on his chest and another dug into his hair, the eyes softly closed as if he's fallen into a trance.

He looks a bit like Sebastian.

Just add a polo shirt and khaki pants.

Muller turns and paces the other way as another corkscrew of pain twists through his spine. Yeats comes out of the shadows and Muller kicks him away and turns and paces back toward the fireplace.

He notices the handsome slave again and thinks about Sebastian and the woman at the airport. Sebastian betrayed his family, lied and deceived everybody, but for some reason Muller can't hold it against him. The charming Englishman is excused, somehow. Exempt from the rules that govern lesser people. Why? What makes him so superior? Is it the polished manners and the fine clothes—or is it simply that bloody accent? He could talk about a bowl of yoghurt and make it sound dignified.

Muller halts before the photo. 'Bastard,' he whispers.

Eliot is quiet, eyes closed. Muller keeps pacing for a while, to make sure he's really out, and then carries him up the stairs.

The bedroom is dark. He lays the boy on the empty bed, between two pillows. He walks to the open door of the nursery and sees Rebekah at the laptop, gazing into the screen, her face glowing blue. 'What are you doing?' he says.

'Checking messages.'

'Again?'

'Yes,' she says. 'Again.'

Let it go, he thinks. Just let it go.

Rebekah's mother flies in for two weeks. Muller's parents visit during the following week. The presence of family has an unexpectedly calming effect. There is extra help around the house. There are drives along the snowy coast and meals at restaurants. Everyone is on their best behaviour. The jagged edges around Rebekah's mood become softer, and Muller feels more relaxed.

He also feels closer to Eliot, who's becoming more than just a baby, more than a swaddled cream-coloured thing that feeds, sleeps, and weeps: he's becoming Muller's son. A bright-eyed boy with a toothless grin. Muller feels a need, like a growing hunger, to hold the boy and dance with him and coo. He needs to read him Hemingway and Wordsworth in the rocking chair. He invents limericks for him:

There once was a brontosaurus,
Whose name was Sir Reginald Morris,
He told lousy jokes,
To his dinosaur blokes,
And they cried, 'To extinction he'll bore us!'

Muller wakens one night during a snowstorm. He gets out of bed, hurries downstairs, and starts shovelling the front porch. It's four o'clock in the morning. He realizes that he must look like a madman in his winter boots and pyjamas, thrusting his shovel wildly into the snow, but he's worried that the snow might pile up in front of the door, worried that he might not be able to get Eliot out in the event of an emergency. He can't take that chance. He needs to protect Eliot. Fatherhood, he's learned, is a form of insanity, a state in which intense love and chronic worry become forever entangled.

But he relishes this disturbing new happiness. He doesn't want to lose it, and doesn't think he can, until he notices the laptop one morning.

It's on the table in the nursery, as usual. It's an old machine, a clunker by today's standards. The cooling fan buzzes like a large sluggish fly.

Odd that it's on just now. Rebekah got up a few minutes ago. She's in the bathroom taking a shower. Has she already checked her messages?

He recalls that she used the laptop late last night—he was the one who turned it off, after tidying up the nursery—so it's peculiar that the machine is buzzing again so early in the day, a galaxy of stars looming out of the screen, mesmerizing him with sudden questions.

He's holding Eliot. He slips a hand free and touches the mouse pad.

The stars vanish.

The web browser appears.

He drags the cursor to the top of the window and clicks on the search history.

There's one item for today. An email account that he doesn't recognize. It isn't Rebekah's account at the university or the account that they share for messages to mutual friends and family.

He sifts through the search history. There are five logins to the account yesterday. Six the day before. She's been checking the account for the past two months, ever since December, when they hooked up the Internet.

He clicks on one of the entries and a login screen pops up. He slides the cursor into the top window. Rebekah's username appears. Finger trembling, he pecks out 'atlantic2001' in the password window—the password they use for their shared account.

It doesn't work and so he tries again, putting the numbers first.

Nothing.

He tries it the other way around again, in case he got it wrong the first time. It still doesn't work and he stares at the blank window. He can't think of what other passwords to try—or rather he can think of too many possibilities. A universe of possibilities, overwhelming him like the stars that start whizzing out of the screen.

Eliot sighs and Muller catches the scent of his breath.

It's mother's milk, sweet as caramel.

If you don't know that somebody is keeping a secret from you, then it makes no difference. *Ignorance is bliss*, as they say. Yet it's another thing to know that somebody is keeping a secret from you, an enormous secret—to know it exists, to realize it surrounds you—but to not know what it is. You discover, then, that things are not what they seem. People say that, too: *Things aren't what they seem*. But now Muller understands. The world contains something invisible. It contains, perhaps, an entire parallel world. He ponders it constantly, and finds himself looking out for it, as if he might catch a glimpse of this ghostly dimension, although he detects nothing definite. Nothing solid. Only a growing uncertainty. A sense that everything has begun to shiver. At times he doesn't believe it, or seems to forget—and then, for a moment, reality takes on its usual aspect. The sky is just a sky. A table is a table. Rebekah is Rebekah. And then he remembers: she has a secret.

The thought sickens him. He loses his appetite. Cockroaches of anxiety scuttle through his body. He dreams of a green pillar towering before him, inscribed with runes that are too faded to read. He tries to walk around the pillar but can't. He tries to turn and walk the other way but it reappears and blocks his path. He tells himself that he's overreacting. Not every secret is sinister. Some are trivial. She might be writing to an old girlfriend, for instance. Why not? And he's relieved at this possibility. He encourages himself to trust her. Real love is radical trust, isn't it? Radical acceptance. A belief that all is well with her, with their relationship, no matter how things might seem.

Trust, Mull.

Trust.

Or is he too afraid to know the truth? That she's in contact with a man. In contact with Sebastian. Not that there's any evidence of it. Not a shred. Besides, Sebastian is already involved with a woman, the woman at the airport, and so it's impossible that he's involved with Rebekah as well.

Or is it?

He knows he's being paranoid, but the demons won't stop whispering. He spends his lunch hours at work surfing the Internet, reading about spyware that will track her keystrokes on the laptop and transmit the information to him via email. He can get her password. He can see everything she writes. It's an easy solution—the truth, the whole truth, for thirty-nine US dollars. Instead he walks into the bedroom one morning. She's reclining against a throne of pillows, nursing Eliot. Muller notices the buzz of the laptop in the nursery.

He glances inside. The machine is on. He walks around the bed and stands over her. 'I notice that you've been using the laptop quite a bit, Bek. Why do you do that?'

'I go online sometimes. I surf the Net.'

'No. No. I don't think it's that simple. I've looked at your search history. You've been checking an email account, an account I didn't know about. You've been doing it every day, many times a day. It's the first thing you do in the morning and the last thing you do at night. You're talking to somebody. I want to know who you're talking to. I want to know who this person is.'

She stares at him, expressionless. He's got her, and she knows he's got her.

'I've been talking with Sebastian,' she says calmly.

He doesn't expect such a quick admission. It almost disarms him. '*Talking?*' he says.

'Yeah.'

'Talking about what?'

'Everyday kinds of things.'

'Such as?'

'We're just friends.'

'*Such as?*'

'Books and work. Parenting.'

'Parenting. Well. That sounds reasonable. You won't mind giving me the password so I can confirm all this?'

'I can't.'

'Why not?'

'I can't.'

'If you can't, there must be a reason.'

'Because it's private.'

They stare at each other. He fears a stalemate. 'I want that password,' he says. 'I'm not going anywhere until you give me that password.'

He takes a chair and sits beside the bed. He presses her for an explanation and she keeps repeating herself, sticking to her story. They're only friends. Their conversations are none of Muller's business. The radiator bars ping softly behind him. Warm air trickles up his back. There are long spells of silence. They've had arguments before, but never an impasse like this, never a sheer wall between them.

'You do realize that today is Thursday?' he says after an hour. 'It's my day off. I'll be at home all day today, and tomorrow, and the weekend. I'm not going anywhere. I'm not going to budge until you give me that password.'

'Alright,' she says. 'I'll give it to you—but not now. I need some time.'

'Time?'

'To go for a walk.'

'Why do you need to go for a walk?'

'There's too much pressure right now.'

'Fine. You go for a walk and then you'll give me the password.'

He stands up and waits as she gets dressed. He follows her downstairs and holds Eliot as she puts her boots on. She ties the boy into the baby sling and then slips her coat on and zips it over him.

Muller takes a coat off the hook.

'What are you doing?' she says.

'I'm coming with you.'

'But I don't want you with me. I want to be alone.'

'You can walk ahead of me. I won't say a word.'

The sidewalks are covered in snow and they walk along the street curb. He hangs back a few steps, trying to give her space.

He wants to believe what she told him—that they're only friends. It could be true. Communication over email might be a natural extension of their usual conversations. She doesn't want to show him the messages because it simply isn't his business—and because he might misinterpret things. Get the wrong idea.

He's prepared to believe her. Really.

If he could only see those messages.

He hurries up beside her. 'Bek, let's be reasonable. Can't we talk about this?'

She stops. 'I need to walk. Okay?'

'Please, Bek.'

'You're pressuring me.'

'I'm sorry. I don't mean to pressure you.'

She starts walking. He follows. 'Would you *stop*?' she says, red-faced.

'Okay. Okay.'

She starts away again. The loose end of the baby sling hangs down from the back of her coat, wagging lazily. A minute later she vanishes around a bend in the road.

He runs after her. His boots are loose and heavy, and his socks slide down his ankles and under his heels. He reaches the bend and scans the intersection ahead of him, then looks to his left.

She's making her way down a side street. He figures that she's going someplace with an Internet connection. Someplace she can delete the messages. The university, maybe. It's twenty minutes away on foot—although probably longer today because the roads are snowy and she's carrying Eliot.

He sprints back the way he came. A row of houses stands between them. He reaches a pedestrian lane that connects the two roads and runs down it, expecting that she's already passed on the other side, but she's approaching, walking with her head down. Eliot is a bulge under her coat.

Muller dives behind a row of trash bins. It's like a scene from a bad comedy. He waits a little and then peeks up with

151

his face caked in snow. He hurries to the end of the lane. She's passed by, she's a few dozen yards away. The road ahead of her is long and empty, hedged with old snowdrifts and trees that are swaying stiffly under a sunless sky.

He steps back and crouches in case she looks over her shoulder. Soon she vanishes behind the drifts. He starts running again but the going is more difficult now. The snow is slippery and his socks continue their downward slide, balling up in front of his toes.

He reaches a gap in the drifts. A path meanders through it, down into a park and then up into a neighbourhood on the other side. She may have gone that way, toward the university, or she may have kept straight, following the road. There's an intersection ahead and she could have gone left and headed back home, or downtown. He has no idea.

After a few panicked seconds he runs into the park—it's a guess. The path is icy and pocked with footprints. As he emerges on the other side he sees some teenagers approaching. One of them is smoking and gesturing carelessly, his hair flopping with his gangly stride like an umbrella opening and closing.

'Did you see a woman?' Muller calls out. He points down the road. 'A woman. She had a, she had a—'

His mouth is frozen: the words are pebbles.

The teens watch him, amused.

He jogs to an intersection, gasping for breath. Birds are perched on a telephone cable. They're waddling sideways like abacus beads. To his right and left are houses and in the distance ahead is a plaza. Storefronts and parked cars. His eyes are blurred, watering from the cold. He doesn't know which way to go. The wind is beating in his ears. 'Please God,' he whispers. 'Save my family.'

He knows the words are empty, pathetic. The prayer of the faithless. Then he sees it—a flicker at the plaza. A flicker so small, like a faint stroke of blue in the background of a massive painting of houses and parked cars and store windows and grey sky. The tail end of the baby sling. He staggers on with fresh determination. He reaches the parking lot and cuts through a gas station and comes to a busy intersection. She's already on the other side, at the edge of the campus.

He crosses at the light and then has to wait for another. She vanishes through a cluster of student residences, but her pace is unhurried and it doesn't take long for him to catch up. He slows to a walk and trails from a short distance, too weary to care if she sees him now.

She veers onto a pathway that leads to a small brown building. The international student centre. She opens the door and goes inside.

He follows her in a few seconds later. She's vanished again, but there's a sign on the wall: Computer Room. An arrow points up a stairway. He climbs up, his legs elastic and wobbly, and finds the room.

The door is locked and he starts banging on it. 'Bek! Open the door! Come on! Open up!'

He runs down the hallway, boots thudding, and finds a lounge. A man in a turban is reading a newspaper.

'Do you have a key to the computer room?' Muller says.

'Do you have a key? The computer room! The computer room!'

'No key,' the man says.

Muller hurries back down the stairs, hoping to find someone who might help him, when he notices another door. It has a window and he spots her on the other side, behind a monitor.

She sees him and gives a wooden smile. A smile that says, Please, let's not make a scene.

He wipes his watering eyes and enters the room. There are several tables with computers, most of them occupied by foreign students.

'I'll show you,' she says quietly as he walks up.

'How many have you deleted?'

'I didn't delete anything.'

'What is the password?'

'Chagall.'

'Chagall, the painter?'

'Yes, but not here. Please.'

'Not here?' he says loudly. 'What's wrong with here?' People start looking up at him. 'We're out for a walk,' Muller announces with a bitter smile. 'We're a happy family, walking on a winter's day. That's what happy families do, isn't it?'

'Please,' Rebekah whispers. 'Let's go.'

They leave the building in silence.

Eliot wakens under her coat and starts crying.

'We won't make it home,' she says. 'I have to nurse him.'

'Fine. Then nurse him. Do it in there.'

He points to a residence building. They enter by a metal

door and find themselves in a bare cement stairwell. There are puddles of meltwater on the floor. Rebekah sits on a step and puts Eliot to her breast. Muller leans against the wall with his arms folded, and listens to the boy suck and gulp.

There are sixty-three messages in all. They go back ten months. She waits in the bedroom as he reads through them. He's sick to his stomach each time he clicks on the mouse, each time a block of text pops out of the screen, slamming him in the face like a brick. But he's steeled against the shock, prepared for the worst—expecting love letters, expressions of passion and affection, oblique references to sexual maneuvers. Instead, they talk about books and films. Food and art. Why Rothko used numbers rather than titles for his paintings.

Usually she writes to him first, babbling away about this or that, and Sebastian makes a succinct, intelligent reply. Sometimes he doesn't reply at all. It really is like their usual conversations.

Muller is slightly disappointed. Where's all the sleaze?

Despite the seeming innocence of it all, a few messages make him suspicious—not to mention the secrecy of the communications. There *must* be more going on.

'Come here,' he calls out.

She enters the room. Her face is flushed from crying. 'I have some questions,' he says. 'Sit down.'

She lays Eliot on the sheepskin rug. He's sucking on a wooden caterpillar.

'Is Eliot mine?' Muller says.

She bursts into tears. 'Yes!'

'Are you sure?'

'Yes, yes!'

'Then what does this mean,' he says, pointing at the laptop screen. '*We've decided to name him Eliot after the poet, T.S. Eliot. I hope you approve.* Why would you hope that Sebastian *approved* of Eliot's name?'

'I wanted him to like it. That was all. It doesn't mean anything.'

'You're sure about that?'

'Yes.'

'Did you have sex with him?'

'No. Of course not!'

'Are you sure?'

'I'm *sure*.'

'You demanded to know who the woman at the airport was. *I demand that you tell me*, you said. *I want the truth*, you said. Strong words, don't you think? As if you were hurt. As if you were jealous.'

'I was upset that he might be cheating on Evelyn.'

'And then he tells you the woman was a former therapy client who just happened to be waiting for her husband's flight to arrive—who hugged Sebastian as a gesture of thanks for all the help he'd given her. What a fine story, and it seems you believed it. How gullible can you be, Bek? Don't you see he was involved with you and this other woman at the same time?'

'I wasn't involved with him. We were only friends.'

'And then he tells you not to trust my words. He says I

have a way of twisting things, and you say, *Yes, I know he can twist things.*

'I'm sorry.'

'I want the truth, Bek. Do you understand? I know that this was more than a friendship. I know it. Were you physically involved?'

'It was an emotional thing.'

'*Were you physically involved?*'

'We kissed a few times.'

'Oh God,' he moans.

'But mostly we talked.'

'You *kissed* him?'

'It only happened a few times.'

'You actually *kissed* him?'

'I'm sorry.'

'Do you realize how—do you have any idea—?'

'But mostly we talked—'

'You actually put your mouth on his mouth?'

'It wasn't the main thing.'

'Answer the bloody question. You physically put your lips against his lips? Is that what you did?' She gives a nod, watching him meekly. 'Okay, okay,' he says with a hand on his forehead. 'This is just. God. You kissed. And where did this happen?'

'In his office.'

'You kissed in his office at the General?'

'It was mostly talk. I needed somebody to talk to.'

'What are you saying? Are you saying that the man was your therapist?'

'No, please listen! You and I were drifting apart. We weren't getting along. I felt like I had no one.'

'Oh! So I'm to blame for your little dalliance?'

'I'm not blaming you,' she says tearfully. 'I'm sorry. I'm really sorry.'

'I'm not interested in your apologies. Do you understand? I want to know how often you met. I want to know everything. *Every detail.*'

'We met every couple of weeks.'

'Starting when?'

'Last spring.'

'When you got pregnant?'

'After I got pregnant.'

'And you met in his office? Did he call you up one day and say, *Come on over*?'

'I ran into him on the bus. We were talking about a novel or something. He invited me to his office—to continue the conversation.'

'To continue. I see. And it didn't occur to you that the invitation was a *tad* inappropriate?'

'I didn't think anything would happen.'

'You didn't think. Right. So you went to his office and started to kiss?'

'No! The kissing wasn't until later. Not till the fall.'

'How did it happen?'

'We were saying goodbye. It just happened a few times. I feel like you're interrogating me.'

'Because I *am* interrogating you! What did you think? Did you think we were having a nice little chat? Allow me to put this simply, Bek. What you did is a *violation*. It's a *breach*. It's a—'

He clenches at the air, shaking his fists.

Calm down, he thinks.

Calm. Calm. He'll lose the moral high ground if he can't control himself.

Exhaling, he lowers his hands slowly, and says, 'Alright. Let's take this one thing at a time. What else did you do? I mean physically.'

'There was nothing else.'

'Did you hug?'

'Yes. When we said goodbye.'

'When you were kissing?'

'Yes.'

'A full body hug?'

'It was just a hug.'

'Did you rub your pelvises?'

'No.'

'Was there groping?'

'No.'

'Masturbation?'

'No! I keep telling you, it was just—'

'Mostly talk? Okay. What the hell did you talk about?'

'Books and things.'

'Things? What *things*, Bek?'

'They were normal conversations.'

'Sprinkled with kissing?'

'I told you, it was just a few times.'

'How many?'

'I don't know. Five, six.'

'For how long.'

'Maybe a minute.'

'With tongue?'

'What?'

'When you were kissing. Did you use your tongue?'

'Yes.'

He clutches his head with his hands. 'You're saying you stuck your tongue in his mouth?'

'I'm sorry.'

'And he stuck his tongue? He actually—?'

'I'm sorry.'

'And what else did you do while you kissed?'

'What do you mean?'

'You hugged and what else? Were you curled up in his lap, or were you—'

'It was when we were saying goodbye.'

'And what else happened?'

'I told you, there's *nothing* else.'

'If there's something you're leaving out, Bek. I swear.'

'I'm not leaving anything out.'

'Look at me. Look at me.' He points to his eyes and says: 'Just look at me and tell me this. Did he stick his penis in you?'

'Are you kidding?'

'Answer the question. Did he stick—'

'No!' she cries. 'Never! Never!'

She's gazing at him desperately. Eliot gurgles. The boy is on his stomach drooling over a cluster of alphabet blocks.

'Alright,' Muller says. 'Let's summarize this, shall we? You went to his office every couple of weeks. You talked. You hugged. You kissed for maybe a minute when you were saying goodbye. You used your tongue. Am I getting the right picture?'

She nods, sniffling.

'And when you talked, did you talk about *us*?'

'Sometimes.'

'What did you tell him?'

'How we argued sometimes. How we'd been arguing more since I got pregnant.'

'And what did he say?'

'He encouraged me to communicate with you.'

'Ah! To communicate! A good piece of advice. Evidently you didn't follow it.'

Heavy silence. Muller is relishing this. She's going to be good to him from now on. He's going to be in total control.

'Do you have any other email accounts that you use to write to him?' he says.

'No.'

'Are you sure?'

'Yes I'm sure.'

'What is the password to your account at work?'

'The same.'

'Chagall?'

'Yeah.'

'Why Chagall? What is that all about? What the hell do you know about Chagall? For God's sake!'

He opens the account and sifts through it. There are a

few hundred emails, most of them work-related, organized in folders going back four years. There's nothing suspicious, although he's too tired to search for long. In any case he's certain that he's extracted the truth from her.

He swivels the chair toward her. 'So tell me, Bek. Why did this happen?'

'I thought I could be his friend. I didn't think it would go further.'

'But *why*.'

'It was an emotional thing.'

'I want the real why.'

'The real why?'

'*Think*.'

'I *am* thinking. I can't think of anything else. What do you want me to say?'

'I want you to say that you were blind. I want you to say you were stupid. I want you to say you admired a fake.'

She stares at the carpet.

He gets out of the chair. 'Sit down here. You're going to compose a message to him. In your own words. You'll tell him I know everything. You'll tell him that you can't have any contact with him anymore. Not him and not that family. Do you understand?'

He stands behind her while she types out the words, much as he said them. She looks over her shoulder. 'Is that okay?'

'Send it.'

She clicks and the message vanishes.

Muller folds the laptop shut and yanks the plug out of

the wall. 'You will not email him again. Do you understand? You will not have any contact with him or that family again. We're done with them. Is that clear? And if the telephone rings, you won't answer it.'

'What if it's somebody else? What if it's my mother?'

'They can leave a message. There won't be any second chances, Bek. You need to follow the rules or we're finished.'

He goes to his study, lies down on his mattress in the corner, and absorbs the hurt. The concussions of shock and dismay. She's been involved with the bastard for ten months. Unbelievable! And to think that she pretended everything was fine all the while—deceiving and lying. Hiding behind a mask.

Muller never thought she was capable of betrayal. He didn't know she had such guile.

He feels used and small and bitter.

There's cawing outside. He looks up and sees crows through the window. Hundreds of them, high up, wafting in the air like the cinders of a great fire. She's weak, he tells himself. Emotionally weak. She lacks self-control, lacks discipline.

Yet even as he judges her, he notices a strange sympathy for her. He understands how she might have fallen for Sebastian. He understands how she could have drifted into the relationship, gotten too close. Muller himself made the same mistake, didn't he? An emotional affair. Mostly emotional. How can he judge her, when every judgement he throws at her comes flying back at him like a boomerang?

He's a hypocrite.

The door of the study opens. Yeats pokes his head inside. He saunters across the carpet and springs onto Muller's chest. He starts kneading at the sweater, pricking into Muller's skin.

'I should tell her,' Muller whispers.

The truth, Bek, is that I was involved with somebody too.

But that isn't quite right. It's more like this: I was involved before we got married. I drifted away from you first. I've never stopped longing for her.

Yeats curls up. Muller remembers the day they got him from the pound. He was the oldest cat, the one nobody wanted and who was going to be put down. He peed in the carrying box while they transported him back to Rebekah's apartment. She lived off College Street in Toronto.

Muller remembers the tiny bathroom and the claw-foot tub. He remembers the French fry truck next door and the smell of fried lard in the summer and the sound of the potatoes rolling in the drum. He remembers lying in bed with her one afternoon, the first time she said that she loved him. He said he loved her too, but warned that they shouldn't say it too often.

'The meaning is lost if we overuse the words,' he explained, rubbing her knee. 'They become shallow. Love is like good writing.'

'Like writing?'

'It's better to show it than to tell it.'

'You think we shouldn't say it?'

'Just not too often.'

She picked at a fleck on the blanket. 'But sometimes saying things—sometimes—'

'What?'

'It can help us remember why we say them.'

'No. I don't think it's a good idea.'

Weeks later she admitted whispering the words to him every night after he'd fallen asleep.

I love you. I love you.

Always when a car passed under the window, to make sure he didn't hear.

Was she right after all? Do we need to repeat certain things to remember them, to make them stick? Maybe words are like anchors: they keep us in place. Without them we drift.

He decides it's best not to say anything about Lara. The situation is already too complicated. Besides, when he considers the facts coolly, he can't help feeling that Rebekah's sin is greater than his own. After all, she got involved with one of their friends. She crossed the kissing line. She crossed the tongue line. Where the hell was her guilt, her moral compass?

Freud was right: women have a weaker superego, a less-developed conscience—and Rebekah is no exception. She's morally anorexic despite the churchy upbringing. In fact, Muller has a hunch that the only reason she didn't sleep with Sebastian is that *he* must have put up boundaries. For this, the bastard deserves some credit. Muller even feels a grudging sense of gratitude, knowing that Sebastian could have done more, could have slept with her, but chose not to. Was it because he respected Muller too much to make him a cuckold? Was it that—a gesture of decency, of courtesy? Or did Sebastian think it was too risky to take things further with Rebekah—fearing, perhaps, that Evelyn might become suspicious?

Or was he simply too occupied with his other mistress, the woman at the airport, to go the whole distance with a second woman?

There are missing details, obviously. There are things that only Sebastian knows. At the same time, Muller senses that something isn't quite right about Rebekah's story. He ought to realize, of course, that any confession, as a rule, is always just the tip of the iceberg. But there's something in him, a kind of willing ignorance, that keeps him fooled. Keeps him blind. Safely in the dark.

He drives to the grocery store to pick up some diapers one evening, and on the way home passes a gym. Lara once said she worked out there. In the front window is a row of treadmills, so that anybody driving past can behold the pantheon of joggers within, bounding under the brilliant lights and TV screens. He always hopes he might glimpse her, but he never has, not in a hundred drive-bys. The sight of her, now, is quite unexpected. She's bobbing up and down in a bright orange T-shirt.

He does an impulsive U-turn at the intersection and drives back up the road. He pulls into the gym parking lot and swerves into a free space, bumping against a snow drift as he halts the car.

The gym window is behind him.

He looks over his shoulder and sees her over the top of the baby seat. She's near the edge of the treadmill line, jogging briskly, gazing down at her console. A shudder of thrill runs through him. The last time he glimpsed her was months ago in a hospital corridor. She'd been with some colleagues and barely glanced at him—her usual behaviour during chance encounters.

He's just as cold on such occasions. It's part of a mutual understanding that there can't be anything between them—and Muller accepts that. He absolutely accepts it, although now, as he stares at her through the frost lines on the back window, his body pulsing with anticipation, it seems rather extreme that they're so defensive in each other's presence. It's been three years since they were involved. Why can't they relax those defenses? And it's possible she feels the same way.

It's possible, although he's not sure.

He's not sure of anything at the moment, really.

He gets out of the car. Keeping his face down, he walks to a convenience store next to the gym. He wanders through the aisles nervously, conscious of the old man at the register observing him in the security mirror, and finds the mineral water on a back shelf. He buys a one-litre bottle and exits the store.

Halfway across the parking lot he glances toward the gym window and catches Lara's eye. He feigns a surprised smile. He heads toward the window, crunching over ridges of ice.

Her face is glistening in the hard light. She has sweatbands on her wrists and holds them against her breasts like a boxer. He cocks his head and gestures vaguely, half waving, half shrugging, as if to say, 'Fancy meeting you here.'

She stares at him uncomfortably. He points to the grocery bag and makes a drinking motion. She shakes her head, looking confused or maybe annoyed.

'I bought some water,' he chuckles, his face growing more flushed. He pulls the bottle out of the bag and pats his chest. 'For me, for me. I was just at the—' He points toward the store, but she's turned to the woman jogging next to her. They're exchanging words, and the other runners, men with damp faces and soaked armpits, are watching him. Muller waits, holding the bottle with a grin, his breath like smoke in the cold air. Lara glances at him and looks down at her console.

Muller turns and hurries back to the car.

He drives home slowly, cursing, furious with himself for being so reckless. What if other people who know him work out at the gym? What if somebody recognized him through the window? And now he's humiliated himself before Lara. She's got the upper hand in the game of ignoring. He's in the weaker position—although he knows it shouldn't matter. God, none of it should matter! He should have given her up, cut her out of his heart, long ago! He glances toward the passenger seat, at the box of diapers, with a wave of shame.

Supper is ready when he arrives home. He's quiet during the meal.

'Thanks for the mineral water,' Rebekah says.

'No problem.'

'It was nice of you. Is the risotto okay?'

'The risotto is fine.'

'The phone bill arrived today, by the way. I put it on the fridge.'

He looks up from his plate. The bill is fastened to the door with a magnet.

'Are you still worried?' she says.

'Worried?'

'That I might try to contact him.'

'Yes, frankly. I am.'

'I haven't. I promised you and I haven't.'

He wipes his mouth with a napkin. 'Thanks for the risotto.'

'Mull.'

'What.'

'I know it's going to take time. But if you've got worries—I want you to tell me. I don't want you to dwell on them.'

'Well, Bek, it's a bit difficult not to dwell on them after everything you did. Do you think it's something I could just forget? And I still can't believe you had a physical relationship with that man. That you actually *kissed* him. I mean if you had only talked, or hugged a few times—well, then, I might not be quite as upset. Not that you should have been meeting with him at all. Of course not! But I might be more understanding. The fact that you were attracted to another person is human. It could happen to anybody. It could happen to me.'

'What do you mean?'

'I'm saying I'm *human*. I understand temptation. But having self-control, knowing where to draw the line—that's the difference between you and me.'

'I'm sure I'll never do anything like that again.'

'You're sure? You think you've really changed? I trusted you once, Bek. I had faith in you. It's going to take a long time to get that back.'

He knows he's being hard on her. He's projecting his own guilt and anger about his own mistakes.

Such is life, he thinks. We always stuff our sins into somebody else's garbage can.

It's April, now, and there's a heavy snowfall. The flakes come down thick and soft like ash, blanketing the crocuses. The next morning it rains and he finds Rebekah standing on the mattress in the bedroom, sticking a pair of scissors into a bulge in the wallpaper.

The bulge pops, and a thin stream of water gushes out and runs down the wall.

'What are you doing?' he says. 'What's going on?'

'The rain seeped in. It's coming from everywhere.'

He notices a bucket on the floor. It's catching drops that are falling from the light fixture.

Muller takes a towel that's draped on a chair and climbs onto the bed. He wipes the wet streaks off the wallpaper, and then peers down between the mattress and the wall. He squeezes the towel into the space and wipes the baseboard.

'We have to watch out for mould,' he says. 'It grows in the damp. It would be toxic for Eliot, for all of us.'

Rebekah climbs onto the mattress. She looks down toward the baseboard, and reaches into the gap. She takes out her hand and looks at her finger. 'Look—there's something brownish. Is that mould?'

He takes her finger and rubs at it. 'Seems more like grime.'

'Is grime different?'

'It's a form of dirt, technically.'

The neck of her T-shirt is sagging and he can see her breasts. They're swollen with fresh milk. He looks at her face, and she raises her mouth.

Plunk, goes a drop in the bucket.

They kiss hungrily. He reaches for his belt and she pushes off her track pants and pulls him onto her. It's their first time since December and they're both starved for it. The act is hurried and greedy like junk food after a diet. Lara flickers in his thoughts, and he narrows his eyes when looking at Rebekah's body, imagining Lara in her place, blurring the boundaries between the two women, relishing the sense of violation—and relishing, strangely, the possibility that Rebekah is thinking of Sebastian. And he's relished this idea before when making love to her, has mentally granted her permission to fantasize about Sebastian and other men, not so that Muller can justify his own fantasies, but because it's another betrayal, and betrayal is arousing.

Betrayal is a turn-on.

When it's over they lie on their backs. Their hands are draped at their sides, knuckles touching.

Plunk.

Plunk.

He moves his hand away. She turns her head on the pillow and watches him. The bitterness is seeping back into him.

'We should call the landlord,' he says. 'The roof needs to be fixed.'

He may not be ready to forgive her yet, but the encounter brings them closer. On the weekend they take a walk into the downtown. The sun is out and the snow heaps are shrinking. Meltwater ripples down the roads in wide wings, like glimmering flocks of birds.

They order coffees at The Tin Cup. They share sections of the newspaper. A woman enters the café and glances at Muller as she passes. She walks to the counter, pauses, then turns and looks at him. She's brown-haired, with a red button mouth like a doll.

She buys a drink and sits at a nearby table. She keeps glancing at Muller. After a few minutes she gets up and walks over. 'Excuse me,' she says. 'I know we haven't met, but I was wondering—do you know Sebastian Ashfield?'

Muller is surprised to hear that name coming from a stranger, and for a moment he's at a loss for words. 'I do know him—I'm sorry, you are?'

'My name is Celia. You don't recognize me, do you?'

'No. Have we met?'

'I was at the airport that night. With Sebastian. The night he left.'

'That was *you*? Upstairs?'

'Yes. You don't remember me?'

'I saw you only for a second.'

Muller's heart is pounding. He and Rebekah look at each other.

'Do you mind if I asked you a couple of things?' Celia says. 'I don't mean to intrude, but—if it's okay?'

'Of course,' he says. 'Please.'

She pulls up a chair. Eliot is asleep on the coffee table, atop their coats, lying in the shell of his unzipped snowsuit. As Celia regards him with faint endearment, Muller studies her face, the small mouth and large eyes with long lashes, like shaded windows. A house of secrets.

'What's his name?' she says.

'Eliot.'

'He's sweet. Looks so peaceful.'

'Always is during nap time.' He puts out his hand. 'I'm Paul Muller. This is Rebekah.'

'Nice to meet you.' She shakes hands with him over Eliot's body, and then shakes with Rebekah the same way, and they all smile at the awkwardness of it. 'So you know Sebastian?' Celia says.

'We were friends with him and his wife. We hung out together as couples.'

Celia registers this fact with a slight nod. 'Are you still in touch?'

'Not since they left. You and him—are you just friends, or?'

He knows he's coming on strong but it's the obvious question, the essential question. She suppresses a smile. 'We're more than friends, you could say.' She lowers her eyes, thumbing the handle of her coffee mug. 'I'd prefer if you could keep this conversation between us. I wouldn't want his wife—'

'I understand.' He glances at Rebekah and she nods. 'We're not in contact anyhow,' he says. 'Haven't talked to them in a couple of months. So you're involved?' he adds, keeping up the pressure, fearing she might try to slip off the subject.

'Yeah.'

'Romantically—I mean, intimately?'

'We are. It's pretty deep.'

'That's what I thought. When I saw you.' He turns to Rebekah again. 'I told you I saw it right.'

She's gazing at Celia. He feels a bolt of satisfaction. Whatever illusions she still has about the man, whatever lingering feelings, are being smashed.

'So you're in touch with him?' Rebekah says.

'We talk on the phone every day or two. We email.'

'How did you meet?'

'He came to me for advice last April. He was thinking of selling his house. I'm in real estate. We ended up going for a drink and he told me there were problems in his marriage.'

'Really? What sort of problems?'

'Oh, you know—it wasn't working anymore. That sort

of thing. He said they'd probably end up divorced—which is what I was wondering about. Did you notice anything? Any difficulties, I mean? Did they say anything?'

'About a divorce?' Rebekah says with a laugh.

'They seemed fine,' Muller says. 'Although you never really knew what was going on with those people. Not on the inside.'

'If there was a problem I would have noticed,' Rebekah says. 'We saw them almost every week for supper. I babysat their kids sometimes. I never saw any signs. Is he still telling you that—that they're getting divorced?'

'He says that's where it's headed.'

'I wouldn't believe him. It can't be true.'

'He came to you about selling his house in *April*?' Muller says. 'He wasn't offered the job in Switzerland until the late summer.'

'He already knew he was leaving the country. He was already planning it. He was looking for positions overseas.'

Muller shakes his head. 'That's what I mean. You never knew what was going on with them—*him* especially. He never opened up. Not in five years.'

'He says the marriage has been on the rocks for a long time. He wants me to live with him in Geneva, or someplace in England. It's always changing. I tell him I'm not going anywhere until I see the divorce papers.'

'You can't trust him,' Rebekah says. 'God, he's lying. What a liar.'

'You sound so sure.'

'He's stringing you along.'

'How do you know?'

Rebekah looks at Muller. 'We should tell her,' he says.

'Tell me what?'

'I was involved with him,' Rebekah says. 'For almost a year.'

'*You?*'

'I used to see him in his office. It was mostly talk, but we got too close.'

'Wait, wait—you're saying you had an affair?'

'An *emotional* affair. It wasn't really physical. I was going through a hard time and I needed somebody to talk to. Things weren't going well between myself and Paul.'

'When did this begin—and just how close were you and—? Did you—?'

'No! I would never have done that. I mean, we kissed a few times saying goodbye—'

'You kissed?'

'We were saying goodbye. It was more like a close friendship. I thought he cared about me.'

'My God. And this began *when*?'

'Last May. We were in contact by email until a few weeks ago. It ended because Paul found out. If he hadn't found out, then, you know. I'd probably still be—'

'He was seeing both of you at the same time,' Muller says, eager to hammer home the message. 'He began with you in April and Rebekah in May. Seems he was a busy man.'

Celia slumps back, closing her eyes. 'I can't believe...'

Muller waits, suddenly pitying her. A milk steamer starts gurgling behind the counter and Eliot jolts in his snowsuit. Rebekah leans forward and carefully unzips the suit a few more inches.

The boy settles.

'Are you married?' Muller says.

'No,' Celia whispers absently.

'It almost destroyed us, what he did with Rebekah. He charmed her. Manipulated her—and pretended to be my friend. He said you were his therapy client, by the way. In one of their emails. Rebekah confronted him about it and that's what he said.'

He expects a response to this detail, perhaps a denial, but she seems not to have heard him and looks at Rebekah: 'You saw him in his office?'

'Once every couple of weeks. I worked across the road at the university. And you?'

'We met on weekends. At my apartment.'

'What sorts of things did you talk about?' Muller says.

'Fancy things. Artistic things. Wine and French movies.'

'Why Rothko used numbers rather than titles for his paintings?'

'Oh my God. Yes.'

Muller smiles. He's loving this. His deepest suspicion about Sebastian—that he's a complete fake—is being proven beyond any doubt. He's exultant, secretly gloating, as if he's scored a knockout punch.

'What else did he say?' Celia asks Rebekah, worriedly.

'I was usually the one who talked. He was quiet a lot of the time.'

'*Silence*,' Muller says. 'That was his weapon. It made you

uneasy, kept you off balance. It's a psychotherapist's trick. You say nothing and the client feels vulnerable.'

'Are you a therapist, too?'

'Yes. At the Rehab Centre.'

She stares at him, her large delicate eyes marked with strain. She looks at Rebekah. 'Did he say that he loved you?'

'We never used that kind of language. But he made me feel like I was the only one. Like there couldn't be any other.'

'But what if there *are* others?' Muller says. 'After all, if he was willing to see two women at the same time, then why not three? Why not four?'

'God, you're probably right,' Rebekah says. 'There was usually some woman or other coming out of his office, just before I'd see him. I always assumed they were clients, but sometimes I had an odd feeling about it—like he was hiding something.'

'Maybe he was sleeping with his clients? Therapy clients can be vulnerable—and his office was in an isolated area. Did you know that?' he asks Celia.

'No.'

'There were no other offices around. Maybe that's how he wanted it? He might be a psychopath for all we know. Or a sociopath. Not that there's much difference.'

'A *psychopath*?'

'The charming kind. The sort of man who uses his good looks and sophistication to manipulate women, simply for the pleasure of it. A man with little or no conscience.'

'I think you're right, I think you've got it,' Rebekah says. 'The man is sick. There *must* be other women.'

Celia draws a breath, pressing a hand to her chest.

'Are you okay?' Muller says.

'I never thought of him that way. A psychopath,' she murmurs to herself. 'I'm supposed to see him in a few weeks. What if he *is* a psychopath?'

'You're seeing him here?'

'No. In Paris.'

'Paris, France?'

'They'll be visiting Evelyn's sister.'

'But you're not going now?' Rebekah says. 'Knowing all this?'

'I don't know. I don't know what to think.' She looks at her watch. 'He's expecting me to call him in a while.'

'He'll deny everything if you tell him you spoke with us. He'll say we're *twisting* things. That's what he said about Paul. He turned me against Paul, and he'll try to turn you against *us*. That seems to be his strategy.'

'You're sure it never went further with you and him?' Celia says in a low voice. 'I mean, you said there was kissing—'

'It was just a few times. Five or six times maybe. It didn't go further—and I would never have let it go further. It was an emotional affair. It wasn't a physical thing.'

'And it makes sense that he wanted to keep it that way,' Muller says.

'Why?' Celia says.

'Because Rebekah and Evelyn knew each other. We were at their house almost every weekend. If he got too involved with Rebekah, then Evelyn might have suspected—might have detected something in their behaviour. He couldn't take that risk and so he only went so far. You see? He was calculating. He knew exactly what he was doing.'

They talk for a while longer, trading more details, firming up their impressions of the man. Sebastian Ashfield is a master manipulator, a smooth and polished liar. Muller sees it, Rebekah sees it—at last she really *sees* it—although Celia remains reluctant to accept the truth.

Of course it's understandable. She got into a more serious relationship with him. It's harder to face the reality.

Before leaving the café they give Celia their phone number, in case she needs to reach them.

'Didn't I tell you he was a fake?' Muller says as he and Rebekah start down the sidewalk. 'Didn't I say it?'

'You were right,' she says.

'I knew it. I sensed it all along.'

'He's going to lie to her.'

'Oh, there's no doubt he's going to lie to her. Count yourself lucky, Bek. It could have been worse for you. For all of us. A man like that could have toyed with you more than he did. He could have destroyed our relationship, our family, without a second thought.'

They circle around a flooded intersection. A car passes, unzipping a tide of water that smacks against the curb and splashes onto their shoes.

'And if there's anything else you're not telling me,' he says. 'You said you told me everything, but if there's anything else you need to say—'

'No, no.'

'—then you need to say it now. Because there won't be any more chances.'

'I know that. But I told you everything. There's nothing more to tell.'

Days pass and there's no word from Celia. Muller figures that Sebastian worked his charm on her.

At least *we* know the truth, he thinks. The man is devious, guiltless—if not a genuine psychopath then something close to it. And yet, despite this realization, Muller notices something troubling. He first noticed it weeks ago, after discovering the secret emails, although these latest revelations have brought the matter into greater focus: he and Rebekah still haven't disposed of all the gifts and mementos associated with the Englishman and his family. Muller should have insisted on it—the mementos, as far as he's concerned, are tainted reminders of all the lies and manipulation. But the objects remain untouched, in plain sight. There's the carved salad bowl with the fish-headed fork and spoon, which the Ashfields gave them one Christmas—it's in the kitchen cupboard over the stove. There are also novels, wine guides, an etiquette book, recipe books, dozens of photographs, crayon drawings by Kate and David, toys, baby clothes, and two cases of fine wine, which Muller and Rebekah inherited because the moving company refused to pack them (the bottles might have broken during the Atlantic crossing).

All of these possessions still occupy the shelves and walls

and corners of the apartment. They call out to Muller every day, reminding him of the Ashfields—of the friendship he vaguely misses. Of the man he still somehow admires, despite all that's happened.

Rebekah feels the same way, no doubt.

Their hearts are weak, it seems. Stubbornly weak and foolish. And he fears there is no cure for that.

He's at the hospital late one day, when there's a knock at his door. He turns and sees Lara.

'Working overtime?' she says.

'Oh. Hello.' He's stunned, hands frozen on the computer keyboard. He wasn't ready for this—her honey-brown face in the doorway. She's in a tight sport shirt, the kind she used to wear, flattering the outlines of her shoulders and breasts.

'I hope I'm not disturbing you?' she says.

'No. I was only.' He gestures to the desk.

'I was just passing through. I was upstairs.'

'Upstairs?'

'There was a mistake on my pay stub. Anyway, I wanted to apologize for being so rude that night. At the gym.'

'Oh that. That was nothing.'

'It sort of took me off guard.'

'I'm sorry. I got a bottle of water at the store and saw you through the window.'

A cleaning trolley squeals down the corridor. He notices Margaret Frye's office through the open door. She's gone for the day. He feels a quiver of excitement, like the moments before an avalanche.

'Rumours are you're a father?' Lara says.

'Ah yes, indeed.' He digs into a pocket for his wallet. 'Here he is,' he says, opening to the photo. 'Eliot. That's his name.'

It's a studio shot of the boy, naked on his belly. 'He's cute,' Lara says. 'Looks like a little whale. How old is he?'

'Almost four months now. Three in the picture.'

'Bright eyes.'

'They're Rebekah's eyes. Rebekah's nose too. He's all Rebekah, it seems.'

'And that bothers you, does it?'

'Not at all. I prefer having a son who doesn't resemble me. Otherwise I might feel I was parenting myself. I might try to fix my flaws.'

'Flaws? What flaws?'

'Oh, you know me all too well, don't you?'

They laugh. His face is throbbing. It's just like old times and he needs to control himself, needs to resist getting swept away. 'I don't think I've ever seen your office,' she says, looking about.

'Yes, this is it. You like the cracks in the walls?'

'Don't expect me to feel sorry for you. You psychologist types are lucky, you know. You always get your own office.'

'It's the nature of our work. Confidential.'

'So when you make a mistake nobody sees it?'

'Actually, it's true—which has certain advantages. When a surgeon screws up the patient dies, but when a psychologist screws up the patient blames himself.'

'And have *you* ever screwed up?'

'I've made a few mistakes. Nothing fatal, though.'

'Nothing fatal. Listen to him.' They smile at each other. 'So how do you do it?' she says. 'How do you fix somebody?'

'You talk to them.'

'Yes, but what do you say?'

'What you say matters less than how you say it. It's like music. As long as the melody is nice it doesn't matter how the lyrics go.'

'Really? So what's your melody?'

'Nothing fancy. Mostly easy listening.'

'Oh, right. You just nod your head and go, *Hmm.*'

'You shouldn't make fun of a psychologist's *Hmm.* It's worth a hundred bucks an hour.'

'Is that what you're making?'

'Not in this place.'

'You mean you've opened your own office?'

'No. I never got around to that. But I'm still writing. I'm working on a novel, actually.'

'What's it about? Wait—I can't ask you that, right?'

'You remembered.'

'How could I forget?'

He checks his watch. He needs to get out of his chair. Needs to *leave.*

'Am I holding you up?' she says.

'I'm fine. Got a couple minutes.'

'Hey, I remember you used to write poems.'

'I've written lots of poems.'

'Can't you show me one? I mean, one that's finished.'

'Well, I'm not sure I'd be comfortable.'

'Oh come on. Please.'

'Okay. Here's one. A short one. It's about writer's block. It goes like this. *My cold fingers clutch and shake these thoughts. Such feeble petals of snow fall.*'

'That's it?'

'That's it.'

'Interesting. No rhymes.'

'Poems generally don't rhyme anymore. Rhymes are like God's miracles. Very rare.'

'What about that other poem? The one you were working on when we—you know.'

'When you and I—?'

'It was about beauty or something.'

'The beauty poem. Yes. I never managed to finish that one.'

'I'd always sort of wondered about it.'

'I suppose I could show you a bit one day. The part that I finished. If you wanted to see it.'

'Oh, I was just wondering.'

'In fact, there's a fragment on my computer here. A few lines.'

'A few lines?'

'Did you want to see it?'

'I guess you've got me curious. But what about your rule?'

'I suppose we could break that rule just once. It's no big deal anyway. Only a fragment. But maybe we should close the, uh, door. Just in case.'

'In case?'

'Oh, you know. Poetry isn't allowed on hospital grounds.'

'You're still the funny boy.'

'No, really. Sonnets are antibiotic resistant.'

He laughs and starts clicking anxiously at the keyboard. He knows it's a catastrophic mistake. He needs to stop everything, needs to reverse gears—but a switch has been flipped and his heart is pumping, his body warm and humming like an engine.

'Anyhow, here it is,' he says. 'The great fragment.'

He gets out of the chair. Lara sits and leans toward the monitor. He squats by the desk and reads silently with her.

'It's a little choppy,' he says. 'I would change a few things.'

'No, I like it. I don't get it all, but I like it. The part near the end is nice.'

'What part.'

'*Man, you are her song. A liquid love tongue, full as the dark evening.*'

'*Languid* love tongue. Not liquid.'

'Sorry. I'm a bit dyslexic.'

'Liquid works, though. The connotation of water.'

She looks at him. 'Was it for me?'

'Yes.'

'You never told me.'

'I was going to tell you. When it was finished.'

'You should have told me.'

'I meant to but...'

She touches his hand. They gaze at each other. She slides out of the chair and into his arms.

They're on their knees. He presses his face into her hair

186

and she smells of vanilla. Of childhood. Of licking ice cream when he was a kid. She murmurs and he rubs his hands over her blouse, over her shoulder blades and into the gully of her spine. He forgot these astonishing contours and the sense of falling apart in her arms. Of being dismantled and rearranged beyond recognition.

He brushes his lips across her neck.

She turns away.

'Lara?'

She gets to her feet. He looks up, confused. She holds her hand against his forehead as if to keep him down—or as if blessing him in some peculiar way.

'What is it?' he says. He gets up and puts his arms around her. 'Lara, what's wrong?'

Through the window he notices the gravel lot behind the building. The crumbling walls of the old British military hospital, catching the crimson glow of the evening light. She slips her arms under his and holds him, giving a sigh. He reaches for the window and pulls a cord.

The blinds drop with a thud.

Lara gives a start, then laughs. 'Shhh,' he says.

They hold each other and sway. 'I was afraid of coming here,' she whispers. 'I was afraid of this. That this might happen.'

'I know. I was afraid too.'

Her shoulders go limp.

'What's the matter, Lara?'

'It's just—the last time was so intense. I want to be careful.'

'We could just talk if you want.'

'But I want to hold you.'

'Why don't we sit? Would that be okay?'

They settle onto the floor. He puts his arm around her, and she immediately turns with a smile and reclines onto his lap.

'I knew we were going to be together again,' she says, gazing up at him. 'I always knew.'

He brushes her hair. 'How did you know?'

'I feel these things. Didn't you sense it?'

'Yes, I did.'

He studies her eyes. They aren't so different, really. If you don't look too closely, they look fine.

She takes his hand and kisses the fingertips and he thinks of Rebekah. She's at home making supper. He sees her at the counter peeling an onion. Lara presses his hand against her cheek and he notices a mark on the inside of her wrist. A small gleaming scar.

'What is that?' he says.

'Nothing.' She slips her hand away.

'What was that, Lara?'

'*Nothing.*' She sits up and wraps her arms around her knees.

'Lara? What's going on? What happened to your wrist?'

'I had some problems,' she says after a silence.

'Problems?'

'After you got married.'

'What are you saying?'

'I've always been sort of—depressed.'

'Sort of depressed? You never told me that.'

'I'm telling you now.'

'Are you saying you tried to hurt yourself? Because I got married?'

She gives him a sidelong look. 'I was mad at you. So mad.' Tears are tumbling out of her eyes.

A catastrophic mistake, yes. He needs to stop everything, needs to reverse. He puts his arm around her, delicately, as if comforting a bag of explosives.

The phone rings.

He tenses.

'Are you going to answer it?' she says.

'It's probably Rebekah.'

The phone light flutters like a quick pulse.

It rings four times and goes dead.

'You're afraid of me now,' she says.

'Afraid? No. No.'

'And you can say it. What you're thinking.'

'Say what?'

'That you can't risk it.'

'I wasn't thinking that.'

'Then what were you thinking?'

'Just, you know. How sorry I was that I hurt you. I didn't mean to hurt you.'

'Well, you did.'

The trolley squeals in the corridor. The cleaning woman. A worm-lipped lady with a hairnet. He rubs Lara's shoulder. 'Look,' he says. 'I wonder if we could talk again tomorrow?'

She pulls away with a sigh.

'Come on, Lara. The cleaning lady's out there and Rebekah's going to wonder why I'm late, and I think we need to, you know—process things a bit more.'

'*Process* things?'

'The last time was so intense—that's what you said. I don't want to hurt you all over again. We need to talk about this. We need to make sure you're alright.'

'I feel like you're pushing me away.'

'No, no. You're misreading things. I just don't want you to end up—'

'You're afraid I might do it again?'

'I don't know. I mean, would you? It looked kind of serious. What you did.'

'I did it with a pair of scissors, okay? For cutting nails.'

'For nails?'

'I was cutting my nails on your wedding day.'

'Oh,' he says with an uneasy laugh.

'I was angry with you and kind of. Cut myself. It was impulsive.'

'So you didn't mean to—?'

'I was mad.'

'But you didn't deliberately mean—?'

'I don't know what I meant. I was mad, I was upset.'

He looks toward the door. Thinks he hears voices.

'I'm getting this weird feeling from you,' she says.

'Lara, please. It's the situation. I do want to, you know.'

'You want to *what*?'

'I do want to be here. With you.'

'Look at me and say that.'

'You want me to look at you?'

'Yes.'

He faces her. She leans in and their lips touch. The phone rings.

'God, I have to go.'

He gets up but she clings to his hand. 'When am I going to see you again?'

'I'll call you tomorrow.'

'Are you at work?'

'No, at home.' He goes to the desk and turns off the computer. 'She's usually out between ten and twelve. Can I call you then?'

'I have meetings until eleven.'

'After eleven, then. I'll try, although I can't guarantee it. I mean, if she happens to stay home.'

'When am I going to see you? Are you free on the weekend?'

He grabs his coat. 'This weekend?'

'He's going away until Sunday. He'll be out of town.'

'I'll have to think about it, Lara. The baby and everything—it's hard to plan. But let me see. Let me phone you tomorrow.'

He leaves the hospital in a panic. He shouldn't have let her into the office—should never have let her into his life! He gets in the car and stares through the wet sloshing of the wipers. The guilt pounds at him like a sledgehammer. Shaking, he drives home slowly along the slick roads.

Rebekah is in the kitchen when he arrives.

'What took you so long?' she says.

'I had to meet with one of the doctors.'

He goes to the counter and pours a glass of water. It slips out of his hand and bounces into the sink.

Rebekah glances at him, sprinkling a pinch of salt into a pot. 'Celia called today.'

'She called? Well, well.' Muller gives a self-satisfied chuckle and pours another water.

'She talked with Sebastian and told him everything that we said. Of course he tried to convince her that *we* were manipulating *her*.'

'Oh, of course,' he says. 'It's just like we thought. And did she believe him?'

'No. But she's having a hard time. It's starting to hit her now—that he's been lying.'

'I can only imagine.' He walks to Eliot. The boy is rocking in a baby swing. Muller lifts him out and kisses him on the head. 'How are you doing, little guy?'

'And apparently she *is* married,' Rebekah says.

'Are you serious?'

'And her husband knows about Sebastian. He found out a few weeks ago and their marriage is falling apart. They've got a girl, too. An eight-year-old.'

'Really?'

She dips a wooden spoon into the pot and stirs. 'Anyway,' she says. 'We couldn't talk long because her husband was around. But I feel badly for her. She doesn't know what to do.'

'Is Sebastian still telling her he's getting divorced?'

'Yeah. She said he cried on the phone when she didn't believe him.'

'He cried! Talk about manipulation! Instead of admitting that he lied, he starts hamming things up. It's disgusting.' He carries Eliot to the window. Rain is pelting against the glass.

'She might need our help,' Rebekah says.

'Help? What sort of help?'

'I don't know. Someone to talk to.'

He watches a droplet creeping down the window, through his reflection. Like translucent blood on his forehead. 'I'm tired of all this, Bek. I'm so tired of it. And I'm tired of this place. There are too many reminders here.'

'I know.'

He hears the clink of bowls. She's setting the table. 'We could move if you wanted,' she says.

'I thought you liked it here.'

'I feel ready for a change. If you wanted.'

They talk about it through supper. They could move back to Toronto. He could open a psychology clinic and she could find part-time work as an ESL teacher. The conversation glows with quiet optimism, but he's anguished on the inside. He has to stop this thing with Lara. He has to end it for good.

He lies awake in the study that night, agonizing about everything. The next morning, while Rebekah is out with Eliot, he sits by the phone but resists making the call, not certain how to break the news. He's worried she might sink into another depression and do something impulsive—might hurt herself again. And another part of him doesn't want to end it. Another part of him wants to hold her, wants to kiss her, wants to grab those breasts and press his face between them with a sigh. Not that he's under any illusions. He's not looking for a relationship. Lara may want that, and he can play along, he can fool himself almost, but what he really wants—the only thing he ever wanted—is much simpler: not sex, not even her body. Just the feeling of being with her. If he could only bottle that feeling. That pure milk of wonder.

He knows he's going to destroy his family. Rebekah will pay the price. Eliot will pay the price. It's already happening. He feels trapped and his heart clenches and writhes like a rodent in a bag. He lies awake again that night, knowing he has to confess. But can he do it? Can he look Rebekah in the eye and say, I need to tell you something? And he's tempted to reveal just a few details about the affair—a small portion of the truth. A sugar cube of truth. Enough to sweeten the lie, make it drinkable. But to tell Rebekah even that much, he'll have to end it with Lara.

Assuming he can really let go of her now. Assuming she doesn't slash her wrists.

Light gathers behind the drapes. It's glowing on some papers on the window sill. A chapter of his unfinished novel. It's a story that he has written many times and in different ways, always about an affair, and always a little too far from his own story—too far to provide any sort of catharsis. The current version is about a blind old poet who dictates his verse through a servant girl who has a beautiful voice. He falls in love with her when she reads back his own words.

At least the metaphor is clever: the poet is really in love with himself. He's self-absorbed, just like Muller.

A cry floats down the hall.

It's Eliot. He's waking.

Muller leans up on an elbow and listens. It's so helpless, that cry. It's so miserable and Muller wants to hold him. He wants to fall down on his knees and cry out with him—and in that moment he knows. He has certainty. Conviction. For the first time in his life.

It's about Eliot.

You need to do this for Eliot—and you need to do it *now*.

He throws off the bed covers and gets up. He heads down the hallway. The boy is suddenly quiet, as if he understands the moment is coming. The bedroom door is open and Rebekah is sitting up and nursing him. She watches Muller fixedly as he enters the room.

'I need to tell you something,' she says quietly.

'What?'

'You should sit down.'

'I don't want to sit down. What is it?'

'It's about Sebastian. Please listen. I need to get this out. We had sex—I was involved for over two years. I should have told you. I should have told you everything. I'm so sorry, Mull.'

He looks at Eliot.

'He's yours,' she says. 'Don't doubt him. Please.'

'Two years?'

'I don't have excuses. I know you might not forgive me,

but I had to tell you. And I never meant to tell you, but—it was killing me. It was going to kill all of us. I dreamed I was covered in darkness last night. It was like tar on my body. It was killing me and I prayed all night, I said the Our Father. I couldn't remember all the words but I kept saying what I remembered, and then I knew I had to tell you. And when I promised God I would tell you—'

'God?'

'—the darkness fell off. It peeled away like skin.'

He can't take his eyes off Eliot.

'Don't doubt him,' she says. 'Whatever you do. I lied to you because I didn't want you to worry.'

'You slept with Sebastian.'

'Yes.'

'For two years.'

'I know it's sick. I know *I'm* sick. But please believe me. Eliot is your son. I did try to have a baby with Sebastian, but it didn't happen. I didn't see him that week. I'll tell you everything.'

The words bore through him like a drill. He turns and wanders from the room.

She follows him to the study. 'Please believe me, Mull. I'm not lying to you.'

He slips his pants on. His sweater. Eliot is crying in the bedroom.

'I understand if you need to go away,' she says. 'But you need to believe me.'

'Of course I don't believe you.'

'I'm telling you the truth.'

'Get away from me.'

He heads for the stairs and glimpses the boy through the railing. He's lying on the bed in a green bodysuit. He's wailing with his arms in the air, face crumpled.

'Where are you going?' Rebekah calls down the stairs. 'Muller! Paul!'

He runs out the door.

He runs for a long time. He loses himself in the side streets. It's a breezy morning and he can smell the harbour—the dank stone and rotting wood. He stops at a bench, heaving for air. A bus pulls up and the doors swish open. I need to tell you something. I need to tell you something. The doors close. Diesel fumes drift over him and he vanishes for a few moments, clicks off like a lamp, and then he becomes aware of the wind playing about his face. He hears the trees swaying overhead, their branches rubbing, clattering, and realizes that he can't grasp what happened between Sebastian and Rebekah. His own memories of the past two years are more vivid—the suppers, the pleasant conversation, and all the rest of it. Nostalgic, innocent memories, like old photographs under glass. The truth rolls off them like drops of water.

Will it always be like this—his own memories brighter than the truth? Darkness brighter than the light?

'You okay, sir?'

He sees a man in a red jacket holding a garbage bag. 'You okay?' the man says.

The words are far away. Muller begins walking. He

has no plan, no idea where he's heading. He only knows that he has to keep moving, has to distract himself from the horror. He reaches one of the main roads and a fire truck passes, horns blaring. He sees a pond of rainwater in a schoolyard. Ducks are gliding in like planes, touching down with a splash. A group of joggers flows around him. He crosses a mall parking lot where the massive snow dunes are still melting, sending bright crooked streams across the pavement, pushing silt and bits of cardboard and shopping bags around the sewers. He meanders through a rundown neighbourhood with peeling clapboard walls and bed sheets in the windows. He reaches a bypass that leads to a one-lane highway. He follows it and soon passes some warehouses, a few car dealerships, and a Chinese restaurant with plaster Buddhas meditating at the entrance. His knees are throbbing but the pain is distant. Transport trucks sweep by, kicking particles into his face. The highway straightens out and the heath lies before him, spread out like a reddish-brown carpet, cluttered with boulders and black ponds.

He wanders off the gravel shoulder and into the open land. The highway is to his left and he slowly drifts away from it, although he never loses sight of it, as if a part of him won't let go of the security of a path, even a meaningless path. His footsteps fall with a steady beat. On the horizon is a row of bald hills, covered in milk spots of snow. He sees a moose bent over a pond. Clouds slowly gather, patching up the sky.

It's raining and dark when he encounters the exit lane. It branches off the highway and cuts in front of him. He didn't plan on coming here, but the sight of the exit, the realization of where he is, triggers something in him. Not hope, but a nudge—enough to bend his course. Within a few minutes he's on a broad road, a main strip with darkened storefronts on either side. Rain glitters in the caramel-coloured street lights and strikes the pavement like hollow applause. He passes a motel and a tavern with music drifting out. A taxi cab is idling by the curb. He turns a corner and reaches the neighbourhood.

The house, number 58, is much as he remembers it. A vinyl, boxy place. A glassed-in porch with a pair of bikes inside, hanging from hooks. It's been three years since he was here—since he drove past one afternoon, just to see where she lived.

He stands on the sidewalk. He's soaked and cold. A dim light is visible through the blinds. She said her husband would be away on the weekend, although it's only Friday. Is Friday the weekend? A car approaches from his right, tires searing against the wet road. As the vehicle passes, its headlights flash against his face and across the side of the house.

A gate is ajar. He stares at it a few moments and then he's walking across the lawn, his shoes sweeping over the stubble of grass. He pushes the gate open and sees a row of flagstones. He follows them toward a light that's streaming into a backyard and flickering against the downpour. He looks around a corner and sees her through a dripping window. She's on a sofa, motionless, staring toward a TV with a mesmerized gaze.

He steps back and looks at the upper windows. They're

dark. He glances about and notices the empty garden, the tin shed. He can see the neighbouring houses above the top of the fence. He turns back to the window. There's a tinge of sadness in her face. Is she missing him? Is she hurt that he didn't call? He swallows and notices a sore lump in his throat. He's coming down with something and wonders if it's pneumonia. Do people get pneumonia anymore? Do they die from it? He sees himself lying in a dim hospital room with Rebekah on one side and Lara on the other. He imagines the two of them becoming friends after he dies. He imagines them becoming lovers as he's often fantasized, their bodies moving under a blanket, a patch of sunlight flashing on a wall, a curtain swaying in the breeze. He swallows. He touches his throat. She notices the movement and looks toward the window.

'Lara,' he says, moving closer.

She recoils, open-mouthed, clutching the back of the sofa. He touches the window. He presses his forehead on the glass. 'It's me,' he murmurs.

Her face softens as she recognizes him. He feels his body instantly weakening, because he knows she's going to help him. He can start to let go now. He can start to feel the pain again, because she's going to hold him. She's going to soothe him.

A man comes into the room. Muller recognizes him by the caveman jaw. Dimitri strides to the window, waving his hand like a meat cleaver.

Muller looks at Lara. What a disappointing pair of eyes. He could never have loved her. Dimitri is walking off. A light comes on over the back deck, illuminating the bullets of rainfall. A door opens and the towering man emerges in sweatpants and bare feet. 'What are you doing on my property? Who the hell are you?'

Lara is sweeping her hand sideways, as if to scoop Muller away: Go! Go!

He turns from the window and heads down the side of the house. He remembers the motel. He could spend the night—or maybe take a cab to the airport?

Buy a ticket. Fly away.

'Hey!' Dimitri shouts. He's coming after Muller, feet slapping on the flagstones. 'I'm talking to you!' he says, grabbing Muller's shoulder. 'What are you doing on my property! You think you can snoop around people's houses?'

Lara runs up. 'What are you doing, Dimitri! Leave him alone!'

'We have to call the police.'

'We don't need to call the police. Just forget about him.'

'*Call* the police!'

'Why?'

'Because this might be the guy.'

'What guy?'

'The guy that we read about.'

'It's not him, Dimitri. Come on.'

'You like peeping in windows, buddy?' he says. 'You get a kick out of that, you little son-of-a—?'

'Dim, this is crazy! It's not the guy.'

'How do you know? Call the police.'

'I will not call the police.'

'For God's sake.' He steers Muller toward the backyard, gripping his arm with one hand and his collar with the other.

'What do you think you're doing?' Lara says.

'Get the phone.'

'I'm not going to get the phone.'

'What the hell is wrong with you!' He shoves Muller onto the sopping ground. 'Sit! Don't move!' There's a spool of garden hose attached to the wall. Dimitri unwinds a length of it and begins coiling it around Muller.

'What in the world are you doing?' Lara says.

'I'm tying him up.'

'*Why?*'

'Well if you'd get the phone I wouldn't have to!'

'I'll get the phone, okay? Just calm down.'

She hurries into the house. Dimitri squats down and grabs his collar. 'What's your name?'

'Muller. Paul.'

'*Mullah-what?*' He feels around Muller's pants. He finds a wallet in his back pocket and pulls it out.

'I don't believe it, you have a baby. This is your baby?'

He turns the picture toward Muller. Lara comes out of the house.

'He's got a kid,' Dimitri calls out.

'You took his wallet?'

'Just to get his ID.'

'You can't do that! You'll get us in trouble!'

'I want to know who he is.' He finds a card of some kind. 'Paul Miller. *Muller*. That's your name? Paul Muller?'

'Dim, just let him go!'

Dimitri tosses the wallet onto the ground. Muller gets up and tries to run and stumbles on the hose. Dimitri grabs him and shakes him.

'Lara!' Muller cries.

Dimitri freezes. 'What did you say?'

Muller sees the open wallet on the ground. Eliot's picture. The rain beating on it.

'I'm *talking* to you,' Dimitri says. 'How did you know her name?'

'You said it a minute ago,' Lara says.

'No, I did *not* say it.'

'You said it.'

'I was being careful. I know what I said.'

'He heard you say it. *I* heard you say it.'

'I did *not* say it, Lara. He knows your name—and he said it like he *knows* it.'

'Dimitri, please! Let him go, let him go!'

He turns to Muller, wild-eyed. 'Are you stalking my wife? Is that what you've been doing? Stalking my wife?'

Muller stares at the photograph. A naked baby, spattered in water and mud. Dimitri is shaking him, and through the screaming and the rainfall comes a vision of Sebastian. The well-sculpted forehead and jaw. The dimple in his chin like the final dent of a chisel. He really was larger than life, god-like.

Muller still can't hold anything against him. In fact, he forgives him. Absolves him. I'll take all the blame, he thinks, as Dimitri hurls him against the wall.

PART FOUR

REBEKAH IS AT THE BAY WINDOW when the cab pulls up. Muller comes out of the back and steps into a stream flowing along the curb. He walks slowly toward the house, stooped under the pounding rain. The trees across the road are thrashing against the sky. She hears the door open and listens to the creak of his footsteps on the lower stairway. He coughs like an old man. She turns and sees him as he reaches the landing. He leans a hand against the wall as he slips off his shoes. He starts down the hallway. His clothes are soaked, clinging to his body.

He catches her eye without interest. He continues up the stairs to the upper floor and she waits a moment, afraid. She walks to the hallway and hesitates again. He's in the bathroom—she can hear the rattle of the fan. She's not sure how to approach him. They don't know each other anymore. A single day has made them strangers.

A breeze is billowing against her. She goes down to the front door. It's open and the wind is blowing through, spitting rain into the entry, spitting into her face, as if the elements are mocking her.

She pulls the door shut and goes up to the bathroom. He's leaning over the counter with a towel draped around his shoulders. His clothes are heaped on the floor, caked in mud. There's a bottle of painkillers open by the sink.

'Do you need help?' she says. 'Is there anything I can—?'

He turns toward her. There's a bruise over his eye. 'Leave me alone,' he mutters.

She waits in the bedroom, watching the open door. He comes out of the bathroom and goes into the study. She's tired but struggles to stay awake, knowing he might need help—and worried about what might come next.

Drops are plunking into the bucket beside the bed. Lines of water are running down the wall, silvery in the light falling in from the hallway. The room will be soaked by tomorrow. The apartment will become mould-ridden. They'll have to move out of here, they'll have to move away from this poisoned place—whether together or apart, she won't dare to guess.

She nurses Eliot several times through the night. She drifts in and out of sleep, and dreams the boy is lying on a conveyor belt. It carries him into a burning furnace and he screams, wails frantically, and then he's silent.

Sebastian offers her a shoebox of ashes.

She wakens and sits up, and looks about, unsure the nightmare is over—for she's learned that there are dreams within dreams, nightmares within nightmares. You can never know the whole truth of what you are. The human heart is a Russian doll of deceit.

Eliot is asleep beside her with his mouth agape, fists clenched.

The room smells dank. The clock shows 7:06, although the light in the window is dull. There's heavy fog. She gets out of bed and the wet carpet absorbs her weight with a *squish*. She walks down the hallway to the study. Pushes the door open. Muller is lying on his side, on his mattress in the corner. 'What do you want,' he says.

'I want to know if you're okay.'

'I'm fine.'

'You don't look fine. You look like you're hurt—and sick.'

He says nothing. She glances about and notices the damp streaks on the walls.

Eliot is crying.

She returns to the bedroom and nurses him. She changes him and goes down to the kitchen. She makes a cup of tea and waits.

Will Muller leave again?

The question drips down on her like the leaking of the roof—a constant tapping against her thoughts, a dark trickle running through her hopes.

She has something to eat. She calls the landlord and leaves a message about the leaks. She goes back up to the study and finds Muller sitting up with a hand pressed to his forehead. 'I know you don't want me to help you,' she says. 'I understand that. But I just wanted to say—'

'Don't,' he says. 'I don't want to hear your apologies.'

He coughs. Yeats is beside the bed, pawing a sock.

'I'm going out,' she says. 'I'll be back in a while. I left you some food on the table.' She waits a little, then adds, 'Are you sure you don't need anything?'

He ignores her, rubbing his forehead.

She ties Eliot into the sling and zips him under her jacket. The first thing she notices heading out the door is that there's no wind, not even a breeze. The fog is still and diffused, more like a pallor than a mist, as if the skin of the world has turned grey, corpse-like.

An apt symbol for her own life, she thinks. Something has to die before something can be reborn.

If rebirth is possible. If she isn't imagining it.

She crosses the intersection and starts down the hill toward the cathedral. She's been inside of it only twice, most recently last summer, when the crypt was converted into a café for a fundraising event.

'Even I'd step into a church for a decent espresso,' Sebastian had remarked.

His words come to mind so easily. His words are stuck to her memory like thorns. She'll have to pick them away one by one.

She follows the iron fence to the main doors. They're locked and she walks around the side of the building. There's a man in the churchyard. He throws a stick to a dog and the creature lopes after it, paws tearing through the muddy grass.

A side door is unlocked, but it's heavy and gives slowly as she pushes on the iron handle. She steps under the stone arch. Inside, an elderly woman is sliding a chair up to a table. She has sagging cheeks that hang from her face like pouches. 'I'm sorry,' she says, noticing Rebekah. 'The church is closed.'

'I need to pray,' Rebekah says, moving under a dangling light bulb.

The old woman notices the scruff of Eliot's head sticking up from the jacket.

'I only need a few minutes,' Rebekah says. 'It's sort of an emergency.'

'I suppose a few minutes will be fine.'

Rebekah follows the woman under a low stone ceiling. They pass through another heavy door and up a stairway. A second door opens into the expanse of the church. Rebekah wanders onto the checkered floor. She gazes up at the columns and the stained glass, and remembers what it was like to be a tourist in such places—the postcard admiration, the snapshot wonder.

'You can find your way back when you're ready,' the woman says.

'Thank you.'

The woman leaves her. Rebekah turns toward the altar, and she thinks about her parents. They claimed to be living out God's 'truth' when she was growing up, yet they failed her in so many ways. They were oblivious to her feelings and her deepest needs. They failed to protect her from the sexual abuse. But she knows, now, that she confused their mistakes in living out the truth with the truth itself. She confused her parents, in some unconscious way, with the image of God—and then judged God to be inadequate.

She confused Muller in the same way. And Sebastian.

And herself. That was the root of her brokenness: she made idols of people.

Her tears are flowing but she wipes her face, not wanting to cry. She doesn't want this to be another emotional moment in her life. She doesn't want this to be another bead on her necklace of life experiences.

She approaches the altar. She lowers her eyes and bends down on her knees.

A quarter of an hour later she comes out of the side door. Muller is sitting on a bench in the churchyard. A tree branch hangs behind him like a comforting arm.

She walks over to him. 'I'm glad you followed me.'

'I wanted to see where you were going.'

She sits down on the bench. Eliot opens his eyes and begins to squirm.

Rebekah unties the sling. She slips him between the folds of her jacket and under her shirt. The boy latches on and drinks greedily. She stares into the mist. A foghorn moans and fades away, and she becomes aware of the sound of Eliot's gulping, mingled with the seeping of old rainwater in the grass.

'There's something I need to tell you,' Muller says.

'I know. You were involved with somebody.'

He looks at her.

'I knew for a long time,' she says. 'I had a feeling about it. Then she called last night, a few minutes before you got home. She told me what happened.'

He rubs his shoe against the gravel. 'She called you?'

'She said you'd been involved. She said you might be hurt. There wasn't time to get into details.'

A crow flutters overhead. A second black bird follows, flapping toward the harbour, where dreary patches of light are showing through the fog. Are they more symbols—the flight of crows and the coming of light? She's been noticing symbols everywhere since yesterday. The world, it seems, is alive and overflowing with truth. The poetry of light and darkness.

A breeze slips through the parting of her clothes, brushing over her skin. The boy comes off her breast, red-faced with a drunken smile. He notices Muller and mumbles urgently.

Muller looks at him. Rebekah passes him over, and Muller takes him into his lap.

'I suppose we ought to begin somewhere,' she says. 'I mean, if you're ready.'

'Yes,' Muller says. He wraps his arms around the boy. 'I'm ready.'

Epilogue

EIGHT YEARS LATER, I'M IN the back seat of a taxi, riding through the English countryside. The roadway follows the gentle waves of the hills under a magnificent, cloud-cluttered sky. My driver, a genial man with a duckbill nose, has been making small talk since we left the village. 'And what sort of work might you do, sir?' he says.

'I'm a psychologist. Among other things.'

'Good living, I'd say?'

'Good enough.'

'There's so much stress nowadays, isn't there? A lot of people need psychiatrists.'

'Actually, I said *psychologist*.'

'Oh? Is there a difference?'

'Psychologists aren't medical doctors. We don't give people pills. We don't deal with bodily fluids. Except tears, of course.'

'Tears,' he chuckles. 'That's a good one, sir. Very good. Very good.' We round a bend and descend toward a wooded valley. There are cloud shadows everywhere, draped on the country like patches of cloth.

'But you do talk to people, don't you?' my driver goes on. 'They tell you their problems and you listen. You help them figure things out. Not wanting to tell you how to do your job, sir. But it's like you heal them with words, isn't it? They say something, and you say something, and there's some kind of magic in that.'

'Yes, there is a magic, I suppose.'

He tells me about his daughter. She's depressed and embroiled in a custody battle. I assume he wants my advice, but I'm too preoccupied to say much. He turns onto a dirt road shrouded with trees. 'So you've got some business with Mr Ashfield?' he says, changing the subject, eyeing me in the rear-view mirror.

'I do. Know anything about him?'

'Rich man. I can tell you that much. Came to Brightmore two years ago. It was a ruin, but he fixed it up quite nicely. Quite nicely indeed.'

'What does he do for a living?'

'I was about to ask you the same, sir. We don't see him much in the village. There it is now,' he says, pointing. 'Brightmore.'

I behold it through the flicker of the branches. A sprawling manor. He received a staggering inheritance after the death of his father, or so I was told by the agency that tracked him down. It raises more questions about Sebastian's past—the past he never said much about, and which I doubt that he'll ever share. My driver makes another turn and the splendid view swings before us. A secluded palace in the woods. It vanishes as the road descends below the roof of the trees, but after a few moments it appears again, growing larger and more imposing. High stone walls, creamy grey and bearded with ivy. Rows upon rows of windows. A house of many rooms.

We pull up to an iron gate. The manor stands across a gravel courtyard. The main building is two-storied and topped with chimneys, but there are smaller buildings on either side, obscured in the dense greenery, creating the illusion that the place extends infinitely in both directions.

I pay the driver. 'Wait here a moment.'

I walk to the gate. Birds are chirping everywhere. I find the intercom, barely visible under a creeping vine, and press the button. My cabby leans out his window, puffing on a cigarette.

The intercom crackles. 'Yes? May I help you?'

'I'm here to speak with Mr Ashfield. It's Paul Muller.'

'One moment please.'

A minute later the gate begins squealing open. A man in a black suit emerges from the manor and strides toward me, hands swinging briskly at his sides. 'Good afternoon, Doctor Muller,' he says with a stiff nod. 'Mr Ashfield will see you now. Follow me please.'

I signal to my cabby. He drives off slowly, gawking at the place. The butler leads me across the courtyard. A black BMW is parked in a corner. A sleeker vehicle is concealed under a tarp. We pass through an arched door and enter a spacious foyer with a marble floor and panelled, cigar-coloured walls. Portraits of stodgy-faced aristocrats hang about us, strangely mingled with carved tribal masks. A staircase spirals toward the upper floor, circling the bronze octopus of a chandelier. An old man in overalls and rubber boots is sweeping the floor by an open doorway.

'Do watch your step, sir,' the butler says as we cross the uneven threshold.

We emerge on a porch overlooking a pleasant garden. There are pathways and pyramid-shaped bushes. A pool mirroring the clouds. Sebastian rises from a wicker arm-chair. His face is a little more ragged than I recall, like worn leather, but the good looks have held up.

'Welcome to Brightmore,' he says.

We shake hands firmly, making a show of goodwill. 'Nice place,' I say.

'Can I offer you a drink?'

'A coffee would be fine.'

'Coffee it is, Malcolm,' he says to the butler. 'Espresso for me.'

The butler strides off. Sebastian and I take our seats. 'Will you be in England long?' he says.

'About a week. I'm meeting with my publisher.'

'About the manuscript?'

'No, a travel guide. A walking tour through the southern Balkans.'

I begin telling him about the beauties of Lake Ohrid. A woman appears at the far end of the garden, her summer dress fluttering, the fabric hugging her limbs. I don't recognize her and reach for my glasses.

'So you wished to discuss the manuscript?' Sebastian says abruptly.

I hesitate. The woman vanishes in the trees. 'The manuscript. Yes. You've read through it, then?'

He nods.

'And? What did you think?'

'You've altered the facts. Altered them considerably.'

'I did. But it is, in essence, a novel.'

'Of course. In my opinion, however—and that *is* what you want, isn't it?'

'Yes, yes. Please.'

'Alright. I'll speak candidly, then. I see many problems in the manuscript, not the least of which is the ending. It's too sentimental. A church scene, of all things.'

'But it really happened. She had a spiritual conversion.'

'And what does that mean, a *spiritual conversion*?'

'It's hard to sum up. You could say it was a sudden and deep change, a complete turn away from the person she'd been up until then. The walls that she'd built up inside of herself collapsed. She saw that it was destructive to split life into separate boxes, each with its own truths and moral codes. She saw that her secrets were poisonous. They were killing her. But once she confessed them and turned away from her old self, the walls were gone and she was free, she was whole—and at the same time the focus of her life turned outward. It was as if a great hidden light had been uncovered, a veil torn away. Her love and concerns were no longer centred on herself but on the people around her. She discovered her conscience, her sense of guilt—and the guilt was liberating. It freed her from the illusion of innocence.'

'All this because she found God? How convenient.'

'Oh, but God was the foundation of everything. She would have drifted back into her old ways without God. Her ego was too large. God was the counterweight. God was the truth that outweighed the lies.'

'Convenient *and* practical, then. But doesn't it strike you that, in finding God, Rebekah has gotten herself involved in another affair? Another relationship of dependence—first with me, now with the Divine?'

'I see your point. But the new affair has worked out rather well. Jesus, she says, has been more faithful than any other men in her life. No offence, now.'

'None taken, I assure you.'

The butler arrives with a tray of coffee and biscuits. He sets them before us and retreats to the manor wall, standing with his hands behind his back, gazing impassively toward the garden.

I stir some milk into my coffee. Sebastian downs his espresso in one gulp. He places the cup on the saucer, gently. 'Did you come here to ask about Eliot?' he says.

'I guess I did wonder about your opinion.'

'What did Rebekah tell you?'

'She's always insisted that he's mine. She said that she didn't sleep with you the week she got pregnant—the week she was fertile. You had the flu, apparently. By the time she saw you again, a week or so later, she'd already been with me. So she was absolutely sure, and remains sure, that I'm the father.'

'And you do believe her?'

'Yes. Although—'

'Although what?'

'Well, I do believe her, but when I really think about it, I notice a small doubt, a worm of doubt that maybe, somehow, she might be wrong. Maybe she got the dates mixed up? Maybe her cycle was different that month and she was already pregnant before you got the flu? Not that I truly believe these possibilities. I don't. As Eliot has grown older, I've even noticed certain similarities between me and him that seem to confirm Rebekah's story—and he bears no resemblance to you, either inwardly or outwardly. Yet, despite the evidence, the worm of doubt has never entirely gone away. I still feel a nibble now and then. I mean, what if it turned out that I *wasn't* Eliot's father? How would I react? Would I love him as much? Would I feel betrayed and grow to resent him?'

'Why not do a genetic test? Settle the matter.'

'I almost did, once. Years ago. Rebekah was entirely open to the idea, confident of the result. In the end I resisted because I wanted to believe, as she did, that everything had been made right. God had saved us, had given us a second chance. You see? I wanted to believe. I wanted to have faith. To submit Eliot to a genetic test would have cast doubt on him—and that, in turn, would have cast doubt on everything. It seemed better to live with a little uncertainty about Eliot and faith in God, rather than to have complete certainty about Eliot and no faith in God.'

'So you've become a religious convert as well?'

'I said I had *faith*, although I wouldn't call myself religious. I am not much for holy regulations and rituals. I don't believe in ceremonies for appeasing God and getting favours. But to believe that life, though a mystery, is no accident, to believe that we were created in the image of another-centred Love, so that—'

Sebastian begins to cough.

'Are you alright?'

He clears his throat. 'A crumb of biscuit.'

'Ah.'

'About Eliot—I think I can give you some reassurance on that point. Rebekah is right. I didn't sleep with her that week. I missed my chance and it was deliberate—but I didn't have the flu. That was an excuse. I simply came to my senses and realized I needed to pull back.'

'Pull back?'

'She had become too clingy. I needed to put some distance between us. I was also concerned about Evelyn.'

'How much did Evelyn know?'

'She had her suspicions, as you seem to have guessed in your story. She probably saw Rebekah in Paris when we passed her near the Sainte-Chapelle. For the sake of caution I avoided meeting with Rebekah the next morning. Of course, the Paris incident couldn't have been Evelyn's only cause for suspicion. She was astute enough to have picked up other signs, although what happened in Paris must have crystallized the seriousness of the threat. It probably grew to plague her mind and was one of the pressures that caused us to move away. Not that we ever discussed it. But we both knew. Evelyn had had enough—and I, as I just said, was growing weary of Rebekah's dependency on me.'

'But you encouraged that dependency. You invited her to try and have a baby.'

'No. I'm afraid that part of your story is inaccurate. It was as much her idea as mine.'

'What about Celia?'

'What about her?'

'Did you love her? Did you intend to get divorced and run off with her?'

'No, although I did eventually get divorced. But that's another story.'

The old man with the broom comes out to the porch with a metal bucket. He puts it down with a clatter and begins sweeping along the mossy stones. I look toward the garden but the woman in the summer dress, whoever she is, remains hidden in the trees.

'By the way, I know the truth,' I say. 'Celia wasn't your real estate agent. She came to you for psychotherapy. She was your client.'

'She told you, then?'

'She told us everything. I know that there were other women too. I've done my homework. In fact, I've got a list of names here,' I say, reaching into a pocket. 'The names of the women who admitted—'

'There's no need for that, Paul. What do you want to know?'

I tuck the paper away. 'Only why you did it.'

'Why do you think I did it?'

'I'm not sure, to be honest. I do have some theories.'

'Theories?' he says with a smile. 'Indulge me, Doctor.'

'Alright. One possibility is that you're a romantic. A truly hopeless romantic, the kind of person who falls in love easily and can't control his feelings. But that view isn't altogether satisfying. It doesn't account for—how shall I say it?—your apparent disregard for the consequences of your actions. Unless, that is, you are a psychopath. The charming sort, I mean. There may be other explanations, but it's these two that compel me the most. Are you a hopeless romantic or are you a charming psychopath? Do you have too much heart, or none at all?'

'Is that why you came here? To pass a judgement?'

'I only want to know *why*. What drives a man to have so many affairs, betraying his family and his friends, ruining people's lives in the process?'

He crosses one leg over the other, watching me with inquisitive calm. He could be a fashion model with his Argyle vest and dapper haircut, cropped at the sides and tousled on top. 'I did it for the same reason that you became involved with Lara,' he says. 'It's not about the sex. It's not about love. It's because getting involved with a person is like being invited into a secret—the deepest of secrets. Surely you can understand? And when you follow that secret to its very heart, you discover something extraordinary. I couldn't put it into words. Dare I say, it's a spiritual experience. Perhaps I'm a religious fanatic, after all? Or maybe I'm a failed poet, like you.'

A fly lands on his espresso cup. The insect scuttles along the lip, rubs its stick arms together.

'You almost destroyed me,' I say. 'My entire world.'

'You almost destroyed it yourself.'

'I don't deny that. But you played a part, and I want to understand that part. I don't hold anything against you, if that's what you're thinking.'

'So you've forgiven me? That's generous. First you allow yourself the luxury of judging me, then you allow yourself the satisfaction of forgiving me.'

'Of course I forgive you. So does Rebekah. We could not have gotten free without letting go of the bitterness and hurt. We hope the best for you, Sebastian. I don't mean to sound sentimental in this, or superior. What we hope for you is no less than what we hope for ourselves—I mean the best and fullest of lives. And if I've seemed judgemental in the way I've spoken, it's only my own defensiveness showing through. I still don't feel I can trust you. I don't believe you're being honest with me.'

'But you believe Rebekah? Why is her honesty worth so much more than mine?'

'Because she acknowledged the wrong she did, and she changed. Which reminds me.' I reach into my pocket and take out a ring box. I open it, and tip a small grey stone onto the table. 'You gave it to her before she went on the pilgrimage in Spain. A token of affection. A way of keeping her close to you.'

He takes the stone and rubs it in his palm. 'I remember this one. Very smooth. I found it on the beach one afternoon. We drove there on occasion, usually on weekends. She would have told you that she was going on a hike, or something like that. Did she confess that too?'

'She told me everything.'

'Then you must know about the cabin—a quaint rental cabin on the cliffs. It had a good-sized bed, a wood stove, a liquor cabinet with some decent Scotch. There's nothing like sex with a view of the ocean.'

'You can keep the stone, Sebastian, if you want. Or you can throw it away.'

'It's my choice, is it?' He holds it up. 'A teardrop of lava. Five hundred million years old. Older than choice, I suspect.'

He flicks it onto the table. It clinks against my saucer.

'You think you're innocent?' I say.

'To tell the truth, yes. But I don't think it—I feel it. And that is all I feel. An irreparable innocence.'

'What if your feeling is misguided?'

'It might be. But feeling is first. You should know that, dear poet.'

'You manipulated people. Vulnerable people.'

'We are all vulnerable.'

'You took advantage of them with your—'

'With my what?'

'Your charm. Your polish.'

He laughs. 'You talk about me as if I'm some kind of superman. Don't other people have their own charms, their own powers of influence?'

'They were *vulnerable*, Sebastian! Rebekah had a history of sexual abuse—'

'Abuse!' he cries disdainfully.

'You played on her emotions, her weaknesses—and you did it to all of them.'

'Don't writers manipulate people too? Don't writers play on people's emotions?'

'But nobody suffers. It's just writing.'

'And what if *I've* been abused?'

'You?'

'Look at how you depicted me in that story of yours. A cold-hearted villain. A caricature from some melodrama. You distorted my character. You fabricated all sorts of things. Events that never happened. Conversations that never happened.'

'But it's a novel. The literal details—'

'What? They don't matter?'

'I was trying to capture the spirit of things.'

'The truth is built on facts, Paul, not spirits. You twisted the facts, and therefore you twisted the truth. Are you so blind? What is the difference, really, between you and me? We are both men of passion. We are both manipulators. But you lack the courage to act on what you feel. *That* is the difference. You're too anxious to do what you really want. So you hide in fantasy. You keep your feelings locked up in your writing—whereas I have lived out my poetry. Why should I regret what I am? I suppose if you had more courage, your story would have gone in a different direction. You might have chosen Lara. You might not have fretted so much about the consequences. You might have done things that other people would regard as immoral. But instead you retreated to your writing. To your Judeo-Christian cult. It's all so pathetic. If you had any nerve you would have screwed her. But what did you do? You pulled your tail between your legs and ran. You attacked me with a novel, with lies—to say nothing of all *this*.'

'What?'

He gestures around him. 'This manor. This place. These actors of your ridiculous imagination. Do you expect anybody to believe it?'

There's a *hush-hush*. I notice the old sweeper. He's sweeping over the butler's shoes. They fade and vanish, but the butler continues staring forward, untroubled by the sudden amputation of his feet. With a few more strokes of the broom he's completely erased, and along with him the manor and the garden and the flashing sky, so that nothing remains but Sebastian, gazing at me with a mild sneer.

Hush-hush.

Everything is gone. Blank. White as paper.

He was right, up to a point. I did twist the facts of the story. I distorted them, crushed them like grapes. I've made wine, not fruit. But I could never have made anything else. I was never much of a historian, let alone a poet.

So I never saw him in the English countryside. I never saw him again. I don't know where he is or what happened to him. Celia suffered years of psychological trauma. Her marriage fell apart. I don't know what happened to Evelyn and the children, or the other women we identified. I don't know what became of Lara and her husband. I doubt any of their stories will ever be told. Secrecy is the mistress of shame—faithful forever.

There isn't much else to say. You have the essence of the

story, the red wine of it, drunk to the end. I hear honking outside, and I turn toward the window and see the geese. They often fly over in the late day, just before the light begins to fade. I catch the sound of their wings as they pass above the house, unfurling on the air, and I notice the children coming out of the woods. There's Henry wobbling along on training wheels. There's Leah in a cloth sling, fastened to Rebekah, and there's Eliot on his yellow bike, pulling a wheelie as he bumps on a tree root. Another wave of geese goes by, a fluttering compass needle under the magnificent clouds, and everybody, even me, looks up.

Made in the USA
Charleston, SC
27 April 2014